I0673768

THE BLYTHE GIRLS
Margy's Queer
Inheritance

THE BLYTHE GIRLS
Margy's Queer Inheritance

or

THE WORTH OF A NAME

By

LAURA LEE HOPE

Author of "The Blythe Girls : Rose's Great
Problem," "The Outdoor Girls on Cape
Cod," The Bobbsey Twins and
Baby May," Etc.

Copyright, MCMXXV, by
GROSSET & DUNLAP

Printed in the United States of America

CONTENTS

CONTENTS

The Blythe Girls:
Margy's Queer Inheritance

CHAPTER I

DANGER

"WAS ever such a hot day!" exclaimed Margy Blythe. "In another five minutes I know I shall melt away entirely."

"Well, if you are any more uncomfortable than I am, I'd like to know how you manage it," said her younger sister, Rose, from her seat on a couch in the corner of the room. "I do wish you would come away from that window, Margy Blythe. You are using up all the breeze."

"Breeze!" returned Margy, as she moved from the window and sank dejectedly into a roomy armchair. "I have yet to feel one breath of air, sister dear."

"Now what are you two grumbling about?" The older sister, Helen, came into the room, carrying a pitcher of iced lemonade and three glasses.

1

"Oh, you angel!" cried Rose, jumping up to relieve her sister of the tempting refreshment. "How did you know that I was yearning for lemonade? Oh, give me a taste—quick!"

"Careful!" warned Helen. "I'll pour it, Rose. You always spill everything—there, now, what did I tell you!"

"It's only a very little spill," protested the younger girl, as Helen returned to the kitchen for a cloth with which to mop up the spot on the rug. "You shouldn't be so fussy, Nell darling. Here, let me do that!" as Helen returned, floor-cloth in hand. "I spilled the beans—pardon me!—lemonade, and now I'll mop it up."

Helen readily accepted the offer of assistance and sank down in a chair near Margy's.

"I'll let you pour me a glass of lemonade, too," she told Rose, with a weary smile. "I feel too fagged to lift a hand."

"What we need is to get away from this place for a while," said Margy, setting down her empty glass with an emphatic bang. "The heat has lasted so long it is beginning to get on our nerves."

"Beginning!" repeated Rose, handing Helen a glass of the refreshing liquid. "It's *been* on my nerves for the past six weeks. If it doesn't remove itself—the heat, I mean— pretty soon, I know I'll do something wild. I feel like shouting at the top of my lungs!"

"Restrain yourself!" counseled Margy dryly. "Can you imagine what would happen if you should give way to your desire in a crowded apartment house?"

"Probably be locked up and sent to several different kinds of asylums," returned Rose, with a grin. "Just the same, I will do something desperate if the weather doesn't change pretty soon."

"Seeing that the last of August is almost upon us, I don't see how summer can last much longer," said Margy. Rose stared at her pityingly.

"You are optimistic, aren't you?" she said, getting up restlessly and wandering toward the open window. "Don't you know that September is sometimes the hottest month of all? Ouch! Just listen to that jazz!"

In the apartment above the one in which the three sisters lived there dwelt a musical family —if one could call the discordant racket they made, music. The Jamesons were six in number, counting the mother and father. The younger generation consisted of four husky boys, whose youthful high spirits ran riot all over the place. They were a nuisance, but in spite of that, their outraged neighbors could not help liking them.

The oldest of the quartette rejoiced in the name of Tobias, though every one, in kindness, called him Toby, and played the saxophone.

The other three, Jimmy, John and Andrew, played respectively, piano, flute and violin.

Now, they were all pretty fair players and rather talented, and if they had not been such complete slaves to the great god Jazz, their music might have been a pleasure to their neighbors, rather than—the other thing! As it was, no one could sleep very much before eleven o'clock on most of the nights, no matter how much one might need rest, and the Sundays were days of torment. Many and varied had been the threats directed against this happy-go-lucky family, but so far nothing—but jazz! —had come of it.

"Some day," threatened Rose, as the antiquated strains of "Mammy" crashed down upon them, "I am going to get Toby's saxophone and tie a bomb to it—"

"And get blown up along with the bomb," chuckled Margy. "Toby loves that saxophone like a brother."

"Well, I have to get away from it to-day. Listen to that discord! Isn't it awful?" Rose turned from the window, hands clapped to her ears. "In just about a minute I'll start yelling—"

"And no one will hear you if—" Margy was beginning, when Helen interrupted with a suggestion.

"Let's go away somewhere, where it will be quiet—comparatively, anyway."

"There isn't any such place," said Rose moodily. "We could take a train out to the country, but it really is too late for that."

"I was thinking of the park—Bronx Park," explained Helen. "I could take my drawing things along and maybe sketch a bit while—"

"Margy and I could look at the animals," finished Rose enthusiastically. "The very thing, Nell. Maybe they have some monkeys! I always loved monkeys!"

"You are one, yourself!" teased Margy, and Rose made a face at her as she turned toward her room.

But Margy was not so quick to fall in with the suggestion.

"I don't know that it will be much cooler in the park than it is here," she protested, as Helen gathered up the glasses, preparatory to removing them kitchenward. "And we will have to take the hot subway—"

"Could *anything* be worse than this?" asked her sister, with an eloquent glance in the direction of the ceiling and the apartment just above them.

Margy grinned and reluctantly got up from the big chair.

"Nothing could!" she admitted, and followed Rose into the bedroom.

The three Blythe sisters were country girls, really, for until after the death of their father, not a great while before, they had lived in a big rambling old homestead at Riverdale, a pretty town on Long Island.

The death of Mr. Blythe had left the girls with only a very small life insurance between them and actual want. However, they had lingered on at the old house, reluctant to leave it because of the memories of their gentle, artistic mother and jovial, lovable father that thronged the rooms. It was their mother's death that had broken their father's heart and left the three girls orphaned at the time when they most needed the loving direction and care of their parents.

At last, pressed by the crying need of money, the sisters had come to a momentous decision. They would leave Riverdale, where they had scant chance of earning a living or advancing themselves in any career they might choose, and move to the city where the horizon would be infinitely broadened, where they would at least be able to grasp at opportunity if opportunity came their way. How they made this move has already been related in a former volume entitled, "The Blythe Girls: Helen, Margy and Rose."

Helen, like her mother in looks and disposition, had inherited also her artistic talent. Helen was tall, fair-haired and dreamy-eyed. Being the eldest of the three sisters, she naturally assumed a leadership that they did not dispute.

Unlike Helen in both looks and disposition, was Margy, the second sister. Margy had dark hair and eyes and a creamy, rose-tinted complexion that was her greatest beauty. Also, she was practical and logical by nature, and in this totally unlike both the quiet, dreamy-eyed Helen and temperamental, enthusiastic Rose.

This brings us to the youngest sister, the "baby" of the family. Rose Blythe was a more vivid reproduction of her sister Helen. Her eyes were blue, but they were alive and sparkling, rather than dreamy, her hair, fair like Helen's, was touched to a deeper gold, gleaming almost red in some lights. Rose was enthusiastic and confident, eager to meet the world on its own terms and conquer.

Such were the three girls who had come to New York only a few weeks prior to the opening of this story. In their fight for recognition in the big city they had been moderately successful, despite numerous trials and tribulations and heart-breaking setbacks.

Helen, determined to go on with her art, had been able to make some money coloring prints, and was looking forward to the time when she might find a market for original paintings.

Margy had secured a position as social secretary with a rich, eccentric spinster by the name of Dorcas Pepper. With part of the money she earned at this employment, Margy was taking a special course in secretarial work which she hoped would advance her materially in her career.

Rose, who was not talented artistically like Helen, and who abominated anything as confining and "uninteresting" as typewriting and stenography, had declared herself at the outset for a business career.

As a first step in this direction, she had taken a position in the Lossar-Martin department store. As salesgirl behind the millinery trimmings counter, she had already been given one increase in salary, and so considered that her career was in full swing.

Such was the condition of affairs on this hot Sunday late in August when the combined musical efforts of the Jameson family drove the Blythe sisters toward the comparative peace and quiet of Bronx Park.

"Better wear the thinnest thing you have," advised Rose, as she slipped a pretty yellow organdy over her golden head. "Clothes are a nuisance in weather like this, anyway. Oh, Margy, don't you look gorgeous in that blue thing?" as her sister appeared in the doorway, ready to go. "You should never wear any other color. Ready, Nell?"

Helen replied that she was and appeared that instant, looking so altogether charming and sweet in a frock of flowered voile that Rose put an arm about her and clung to her for a moment.

"You look so much like mother sometimes, Nell, that it makes me feel—funny," she said softly, then laughed very, very gayly to hide the fact that her eyes were wet.

They went downstairs arm in arm and out into the burning heat of the street. As they walked toward the corner they could still hear the blare of the "Jameson brass band" in the apartment over theirs.

The cool shadows of the park were a welcome relief to them after the hot ride up in the subway, and Helen's eyes began to gleam with anticipations as view after beautiful view opened up before them, exquisite bits of background and color, tempting the skill of her brush and pencil.

Rose was leading the way straight toward the animals. Margy threw herself gayly into the happy mood of her younger sister and kept close at her heels. Helen, stifling her own longings for the present, sighed and followed.

For an hour after that she allowed herself to be led from one enclosure to another, exclaiming over the beauty of the pet peacock, laughing at the clumsiness of old bruno, lumbering over rocks in a minature forest, commenting admiringly upon the ability of Jocko, a monkey, to hang for hours at a time head downward and suspended by his tail, while all the time her soul was longing for a quiet spot in the park where she might sit and drink in the beauty all about her, transferring some of it, perhaps, to her beloved canvas.

Suddenly she felt a grip upon her arm, heard Margy's voice, startled, strained:

"Helen—look at the child! Oh, she will be killed!"

CHAPTER II

The Rescuer Rescued

At the words Margy was gone, to be lost almost instantly among the crowd that milled about the cages. Helen, turning to find Rose and drag her away from eager contemplation of a baby bear, found that Margy had disappeared as completely as though the earth had opened and swallowed her up.

"Rose, there is something wrong with Margy!" cried Helen frantically. "We must find her. Oh, where, where is she?"

Meanwhile Margy was having a new and terrifying experience. From her place beside Helen she had seen a small child, who had evidently strayed from its parents without their knowledge. It had been standing quite alone on the edge of a little grotto and before it bulked a huge shape—some animal evidently escaped from the fenced-in enclosures. Margy caught sight of a magnificent lowered head, armed with antlers, of forefoot pawing the ground, and started swiftly to the rescue.

11

She had no plan of action—had not given a thought to what she would do when she reached the spot. All she knew was that that baby, that little, chubby, wide-eyed youngster, must be rescued at any cost.

Her wild dash through the crowd seemed to attract little attention, and when she reached the spot of danger she found that, as yet, no one had realized the little tot's peril. This was not strange, since the place was half hidden by a clump of trees from the rest of the park.

Margy brought herself up short, panting, gasping. There before her the tableau remained unchanged—exactly as she had first glimpsed it.

A giant bull moose, freed by some accident from its enclosure, stood with lowered head, foot angrily pawing the ground, while before him, wide-eyed and eagerly interested, stood a tiny, tow-headed child of three or four.

As Margy stood there, paralyzed with fear for the child, trying to settle upon a course of action, the youngster held out a grubby little hand filled with sticky candy.

"Want some can'y?" he piped, and took a step toward the moose.

Words and action seemed to anger the animal. He took a slow step forward, head swinging slowly from side to side.

Margy stopped no longer to think. With a gasping cry she sprang forward, seized the

child by the arm and flung it with all her force
backward, out of danger.

Not till then had she given a thought to her
own peril. But now, as eager hands grasped
the child and cries of fright began to arise from
the awakened crowd, Margy knew herself in
danger of her life.

The great moose, unused to his freedom, had
been nonplussed by the little child—more nervous than angered. But with Margy it was different. Here was a real enemy, some one who
faced him with blazing eyes, who dared to stand
directly in his path.

With a swift movement the animal lowered
his antlered head and charged.

Margy turned, tried to run, found herself, as
in a terrible dream, powerless to move. In
another moment the moose would be upon her,
goring her with his sharp antlers, trampling
her with his hoofs. She tried to cry out, but
only a strangled moan came from between her
stiff lips.

Then suddenly there was a shout. As in a
daze she saw a figure flash by her, brandishing
something wildly over its head. She closed her
eyes and waited, tried once more to force her
numbed limbs to action and failed.

Suddenly she felt herself caught up by the
sudden onrush of the crowd and carried on, not
away from the moose, but toward it.

She opened her eyes then and dazedly took

in the scene. The great moose, so terrifying
only a moment before had turned and was re-
treating, reluctantly but surely, while behind
him a young man ran, gesticulating and shouting and waving a cane wildly above his head.

Even while Margy watched, two men in uni-
form rushed by her, overtook moose and noisy
pursuer and immediately took charge of the escaped animal.

Margy, surrounded by the frantic, excited
crowd and pushed forward by it, felt herself
grow suddenly weak and faint. She wanted to
sit down somewhere, anywhere, just so that she
might recover her breath and fight down the
dizziness in her head.

The young man with the cane was returning.
He smiled at Margy and immediately rescued
her from the crowd.

"Let's get out of this," he whispered.
"Something tells me you would like to shake
this crazy mob."

Margy nodded dumbly. She permitted the
young man to lead her away, not even questioning the propriety of allowing a total stranger to
take charge of her in this masterful manner.
Anyway, she told herself, fighting off the dizziness in her head, he was not really a stranger,
since he had probably just saved her life. Such
an action was generally considered a pretty
good introduction.

Ultimately she found herself in a quiet part

of the park, where a breath of cool breeze
fanned her hot face and combated the dizziness
in her head.

She glanced up and found her new acquaintance smiling pleasantly down upon her. He
was good looking, in a whimsical, humorous
way. He had blue eyes and sandy hair, a spat-
tering of freckles, and a wide mouth that
laughed easily.

"I'm Dale Elton," he introduced himself
gravely. "And I earn my daily bread by writ-
ing no-account stories for the *Evening Star*.
Now that you know all about me," he added,
with a whimsical gesture toward the bench,
"do you mind if I sit beside you?"

Margy smiled and began to recover her com-
posure.

"I would be very ungrateful not to allow you
that much," she told him. "You saved my life,
you know."

Dale Elton beamed upon her.

"So, I did, didn't I?" he said whimsically.
"It will make an unusual story. 'Gallant girl
rescues child. Daring, unknown reporter
dashes into the picture and rescues rescuer!"

"Oh, but you don't really mean to write it
up!" Margy moved a little closer to him in her
earnestness. "You—you wouldn't put it in the
paper?"

The journalist stared at her in surprise.

"Why not?" he asked. "Wouldn't you like

your picture in the paper with the story of a gallant rescue?"

"I certainly would not!" she flamed at him. "It would make me feel like—like—an idiot. Anyway," she continued more calmly, "you don't look like the kind of person that would do a thing like that when you were asked not to."

Dale Elton stared at her a moment longer, sighed heavily and grinned.

"Lady, you strike me in a tender spot—my chivalry," he mourned. "Reporters aren't supposed to have any, and I can see right here I will have to get rid of it if I intend to succeed in my chosen profession."

"But you promise—you won't put it in the paper?" Margy insisted.

The young man nodded reluctantly.

"I'll have to, if you ask it. You see, that's the kind of fellow I am."

"I think you are rather nice," Margy told him frankly. "Which reminds me," she added, "that I haven't thanked you—for what you did."

The young fellow looked pleased but shrugged his shoulders as though to dismiss any heroic action on his part.

"That moose was more scared and bewildered than anything else," he said. "When I came along waving the old stick, he was glad of an excuse to leave the field. You were great though," he added, with honest admiration. "I never saw anything better than the way you yanked that little shaver out of harm's way. That's why I'd like to write you up,'' he added longingly. ''Quite sure you won't change your mind?''

Margy shook her head and got abruptly to her feet.

''I don't know what I have been thinking of to sit here all this time!'' she exclaimed. ''Helen and Rose will think something dreadful has happened to me.''

''And when they find you with me they will know it has,'' countered the young man, with a grin. ''May I inquire as to the identity of Helen and Rose?''

''My sisters,'' Margy informed him briefly.

She started off quickly in the direction she supposed they had come while Dale Elton kept step beside her.

''If my company becomes obnoxious to you at any time, just tell me,'' he begged her. ''I would take myself off now only that I have a desire to see you once more safe with your friends before I leave you—perhaps to the mercies of another bull moose.''

''Indeed, you mustn't thing of 'taking yourself off' until you have met my sisters,'' Margy told him, smiling. ''They would never forgive me if I let you go before giving them a chance to thank you.''

''Now listen to me, Miss—''

"Blythe," Margy obliged him.

"Miss Blythe," repeated Dale Elton, pausing
and regarding her anxiously. "I will be very
glad indeed to meet your sisters, but I posi-
tively refuse to be thanked. You may not have
guessed it, but I am an extremely modest young
man—"

He was interrupted by a glad cry as a figure
in yellow organdy darted through the crowd.
The next moment Margy was caught in a
smothering embrace.

"Margy, Margy, we thought you had been
hurt or kidnapped or something! We've been
just about scared to death!"

CHAPTER III

An Old Friend

DALE ELTON stood by, smiling amusedly, while the three sisters talked excitedly, Rose and Helen asking a score of questions and Margy doing her best to answer them.

It was Margy who finally tore herself away from them and presented Dale Elton. Helen and Rose had heard enough of the story to appreciate the young man's part in it and so greeted him cordially.

When they started to thank him for his share in the rescue of Margy the young journalist promptly and slyly changed the subject by suggesting that they find the nearest place of refreshment, where they could rest, and have some ice-cream.

The invitation was accepted without hesitation. Even Helen seemed completely won by the pleasant, whimsical manner of their new acquaintance. Before they had reached the little outdoor stand where cold drinks, cake and ice-cream were served, Helen found, to her surprise, that she had told Dale Elton something of her artistic longings and her ambition to paint some of the scenes in the park.

"You ought to find plenty of material here," he said, finding seats for them at a small round table. "You will have to have a permit, though. You know that, don't you?"

Helen looked startled.

"I didn't," she admitted. "I thought the park was free to artists."

"What would they do to her if they found her painting without a permit?" asked Rose impishly.

Dale Elton turned his good-humored smile upon her.

"Nothing very terrible, I guess," he said. "Probably a request to keep off the park scenery until she had secured a permit would be the extent of the punishment."

"How do you go about getting one—a permit, I mean?" asked Helen. "You see," she added, apologetically, "we haven't lived in New York long enough to know our way about very well. Out on Long Island the scenery is free, you know!"

"I don't know just where you would apply for a permit," responded Dale Elton thoughtfully. "I tell you what I'll do, though," he added. "I have an artist friend and I'll get the particulars from him, if you like. It will give me a good excuse to call," this, with a laughing look at Margy.

The latter flushed a little but met his glance calmly.

"You really don't need an excuse, you know, after what you did to-day," she told him, and her tone was so matter-of-fact that Rose afterward declared that, much as she loved her sister, at that moment she could have shaken her with a good will! Here was a good-looking, attractive young man who was evidently very much taken with Margy, and she treated him as though he were the most casual acquaintance. Just after he had saved her life, at that!

They made merry over the French ice-cream and cakes ordered by Dale Elton and only reluctantly left the place when it was evident they would be able to consume no further refreshment for the next few hours at least.

Their new acquaintance escorted them to the subway station and there drew Margy aside. He had taken a notebook from his pocket and was holding a pencil poised suggestively over it.

"Your address, please!" he requested. "You said that I might call and I don't intend to let you take that statement back."

"I don't intend to try," Margy told him, with an answering smile, and gave him the address. It was amazing the feeling she had of having known this Dale Elton always! "You have been very kind to me to-day and I want the opportunity of really thanking you."

The young fellow looked startled.

"Look here!" he protested. "If you are going to start thanking me all over again, I won't come!"

Margy laughed gayly and started after Helen and Rose.

"Oh, very well," she agreed. "I promise never to thank you for anything!"

"I say, Miss Blythe!" Dale Elton was at her elbow again to the annoyance of several people who were trying to shove into the subway entrance. "You haven't changed your mind, have you?" His tone was wistful and Margy glanced at him in surprise.

"About what?" she asked.

"About the story? It's such a pippin. Make me solid with the good old paper. Might even make my fortune. You wouldn't stand in the way of a poor working boy, would you?"

Margy laughed and Rose giggled irrepressibly.

"Don't be so hard-hearted, Margy," urged the latter. "Can't you see how bad he feels?"

Margy chuckled again but shook her head firmly.

"You promised," she reminded the young reporter. "And you don't look like a person who would go back on his word!"

"I'm not," said Dale Elton, mournfully. "That's just the worst of it. It's awful to have been born too good!"

The sisters giggled all the way to the subway
train and almost all the way home at the memory of those mournful words.

And, somehow, despite Margy's perilous experience, the outing seemed to have done them
a world of good. The apartment was as hot as
ever when they reached it and the musical
Jamesons overhead were still grinding out
syncopated tunes, but these annoyances no
longer seemed important.

"You don't know luck when it stares you in
the face, Margy Blythe," said Rose, as she
flung off her hat and fluffed her bright hair
about her face. "Just think of that perfectly
nice Dale Elton wanting to put your picture in
the paper! Why, you would be a regular heroine!"

"If you would tell me what particular good
that would do me, I'd be much obliged to you,"
said Margy dryly, as she repaired to the kitchen
where Helen was already busy with preparations for dinner.

"But aren't you a little bit excited about
Dale Elton?" asked Rose, following and putting an arm about her. "Don't you think he is
perfectly spiffing?"

"Whatever that may be!" retorted Margy,
and Rose lifted both hands in a gesture of de-
spair.

"You are perfectly hopeless, Margy Blythe,"
she cried. "I believe you care more for your

career and your crotchety old Miss Pepper
than you do for all the nice Dale Eltons in the
world!''

''I certainly do!'' returned Margy, and
laughed at the pitying look on the face of her
younger sister. ''You think I'm a funny old
thing and you are just about to wash your
hands of me, aren't you, Rose darling?'' she
asked, as she energetically got out cloth and
silver and began to set the table.

''I think you are a perfect old peach,'' returned Rose, adding gravely after the manner
of a certain Mr. Beadle at the Lossar-Martin
department store. ''But you certainly do fail
to make the most of your opportunities, Miss
Blythe!''

''Dale Elton, for instance?'' asked Margy,
and began to laugh. She kept on laughing till
her merriment grew so infectious that Helen
joined in, and then Rose.

In the midst of it all the bell rang a sudden,
sharp summons and the girls looked at each
other, startled back to gravity.

''Now who can that be?'' cried Helen. ''You
girls don't expect any one to-night, do you?''

They answered in the negative and Rose
reached for the button that released the catch
on the door downstairs.

''Maybe it's Dale Elton,'' she suggested, as
she started toward the hall. ''Speaking of
angels—''

Margy and Helen heard her fling the door open, heard a thin voice inquire: "Does Miss Margy Blythe live here?"

Then the voice of Rose in delighted welcome:

"Miss Jellicoe! My, won't the girls be glad to see you! Come in, do!"

CHAPTER IV

The Delayed Letter

In the kitchen Margy and Helen stared at each other for the space of a second. Then, with one accord, they dried their hands hastily on a towel and made a rush for the front room.

There they found a little old lady, carefully dressed in black silk with a tiny rosebud nestling in the creamy lace about her throat. She was a very old lady indeed, but for all that, the pink of the rosebud was no rosier than the flush in her wrinkled old face and her eyes were as bright as a girl's.

Rose had already relieved her of hat and cloak, and now Margy and Helen flung themselves down on the couch beside her, eager young arms encircling her hungrily.

"Oh, but you look like home!" cried Helen eagerly. "Miss Jessica Jellicoe, how did you know we wanted to see you so badly?"

"And you look just as you always did when you used to come over in the afternoon to—to chat with mother," said Margy, holding one of the withered old hands tight in her own.

"And then you would stay to dinner and afterward you and daddy would play chess while mother began to get the tea and cake ready! Do you remember?" asked Rose breathlessly, and Miss Jessica Jellicoe, looking from one eager, fresh young face to another, felt her old eyes film over with tears and grow dim with pity.

For Miss Jessica Jellicoe had lived neighbor to the Blythes for a number of years and had been a frequent visitor at the old homestead where the mother of these girls had made all welcome. She felt an attachment for Helen and Margy and Rose that could hardly have been stronger had she claimed blood relationship with them. So it was not strange that her old heart should be warmed by this eager reception of her, showing, as it did, the undisguised affection with which the three sisters regarded her.

"Do I remember!" she said in answer to the question of the younger girl. "As though I could ever forget those days, my dear!" She paused and sniffed the air with the suspicion of an old housekeeper. "Something's burning!" she said. "Smells like steak—"

With a startled cry Helen rushed from the room. She pulled the blackened steak from the stove and regarded it tragically. She looked up to find Rose at her elbow.

"Is it spoiled?" whispered the latter and, at

Helen's discouraged nod, added soothingly:
"Don't worry. I can slip out to the delicatessen, if you like."

"Oh, Rose, would you, dear? Oh, and,
Rose," as the latter turned to leave the room,
"don't get pickled pigs' feet and onion salad,
the way you did last time. I've a notion Miss
Jellicoe wouldn't appreciate that combina-
tion!"

Rose made a laughing face at her sister and
the next moment Helen heard the door close
after her.

Rose displayed her growing common sense
by returning a short time later with a really
tempting collection of delicatessen products.
So that, in spite of the mishap to the steak, the
dinner was a merry and successful one. Miss
Jessica Jellicoe was as jolly as any girl herself and even insisted upon helping "clean up"
after the meal.

They had a great deal of fun over it, and
the girls were in such high spirits that they
were totally unprepared for the gravity of the
mood that suddenly descended upon their guest.

They had repaired to the living room and
were telling anecdotes of Riverdale days when
Miss Jellicoe suddenly reached for her hand
bag, which she had placed on the piano, and
from it drew forth a letter.

"I have a sort of surprise for you," she told
the girls, who were watching her curiously. "I

didn't like to tell you before, because I wasn't
a bit sure it would be a pleasant—"

"A surprise!" interrupted Rose joyfully.
"Oh, what a lark!"

"Maybe it is, and then again maybe it isn't,"
warned the little old lady, with a gravity of expression that further mystified her listeners.
"Here it is."

She produced a long, legal looking envelope
from her bag and handed it to Helen.

"A letter!" chortled Rose.   "Open it,
Helen, before I die of curiosity!"

"But I should have received this letter long
ago," cried Helen, bewildered. She glanced
from the letter in her hand to her visitor. "The
postmark dates back several months."

Miss Jessica Jellicoe nodded assent.

"That was the queer part of it," she explained. "The letter was sent to you months
ago, but it was left in that old mail box a piece
down the road from your house where you used
to have your mail delivered before you had the
new mail box put on your house."

"But we haven't used that box for years!"
marveled Margy.

"What made you think to look in it?" asked
Rose eagerly.

The visitor shook her head and a pleasant
smile wreathed her sweet old lips.

"Maybe 'twas fate, or maybe 'twas just
plain hunch," she replied. "I was passing, the

rusty door of the box stood open just a crack, and I thought I'd look in. It was just as well that I did so, too, for I found that letter. Seemed like it had been there a right smart while.''

"It must have been there for a considerable time before we gave up the old house and left Riverdale,'' nodded Helen. "I can't imagine—''

"Oh, open it, Nell, do, before I die of curiosity!'' begged Rose plaintively. "I suppose folks do actually die of curiosity now and then,'' she added naively.

Helen started to rip open the envelope, paused and stared for a moment incredulously at Miss Jellicoe.

"Why this isn't addressed to me! It's for Margy!'' she cried.

Margy reached over and took the letter from her.

"Helen Blythe, don't you know there is a penalty for opening other people's mail?'' she said severely.

Helen's answer was to come closer and peer over Margy's shoulder while Rose hovered eagerly in the rear.

"Margy, I faint! I die!'' Rose cried, in mock agony. "Will you read that letter, or must I?''

"I'd just like to see you try it!'' replied Margy grimly.

Her eyes traveled swiftly down the typewritten page, lingered for a moment on the signature, "J. Jones, Attorney." Then she put down the letter and glanced quietly from her sisters to Miss Jellicoe.

"Aunt Margy Blythe is dead!" she said.

CHAPTER V

A New Tyrant

AFTER Margy's announcement her sisters stared at her for a moment in a startled and bewildered silence. Rose was the first to speak.

"Aunt Margy Blythe!" she repeated wonderingly. "Why, I had almost forgotten there was such a person."

Helen answered with an impatience unusual to her.

"You would hardly remember her, Posie," she said.

Posie was the nickname given to Rose by her friends in the Lossar-Martin department store and the title had clung to the younger girl and followed her into her own home. One would have to look at Rose but once, at her golden hair, her flushed cheeks and laughing eyes to realize how perfectly the descriptive nickname fitted her.

"Aunt Margy Blythe lived in Pogartown, Iowa, and she never went anywhere to see anyone," Helen continued. "I have heard mother say she was an old maid and very eccentric."

"But what does she say—"

"*She* doesn't say anything, but her lawyer does," returned Margy dryly. "Listen!"

They obeyed her breathlessly while Margy read the brief, clear-cut phrases of Mr. J. Jones, Attorney.

"Miss Margaret Blythe,
Riverdale, Long Island.
Dear Madam:

"Your aunt, Margaret Blythe, died in her home in Pogartown, Iowa, on the last day of April. Funeral was private, by her order. We are not sure of your present address and will be greatly obliged if you will let us know where we can reach you at the earliest possible date. We have an important communication for you which cannot be delivered until we make certain of your present address.

"A prompt response would greatly oblige,
"Yours respectfully,
"J. JONES, *Attorney.*'

Margy put down the letter and stared at her sisters. Rose was breathing quickly, as though she had been running, and Helen's cheeks were flushed to an unusually bright pink.

Suddenly Miss Jessica Jellicoe, all but forgotten in her post of observation in the big leather armchair, brought her hands together with a smart clap and chuckled delightedly.

"I told you it was the hand of Fate that

prompted me to open that old letter box!'' she said.

This observation seemed to break the spell of silence that bound the girls and they began to chatter excitedly and all at once. As the voice of Rose was the loudest of all, she eventually, by sheer force of lung power, gained the floor.

"But how do we know it's good news that old lawyer is sending us, anyway?" she cried. "If our poor departed aunt was peculiar as you say—"

"She probably left me her pet canary!" finished Margy.

"J. Jones would hardly call a pet canary an 'important communication'," Helen pointed out to them, her excitement growing. "Poor Aunt Margy may have been queer, but that doesn't say her lawyer would have to be, too."

"Like master, like man," murmured Rose irrepressibly.

"And, on the other hand, I may be heiress to millions," retorted Margy airily. "Who knows?"

"I do!" exclaimed Rose, ruthlessly puncturing this delightful air castle. "Aunt Margy Blythe may have been peculiar, but she couldn't have been as peculiar as all that!"

"No one knew exactly how much Aunt Margy had."

Helen spoke quietly, but the girls and Miss Jellicoe turned to her with instant attention.

She was staring past them, out at the dark patch of night beyond the window.

"I remember having heard mother say once, when I was a little thing, that Aunt Margy Blythe was extraordinarily close with her money. She never had a very large income, but folks who knew her well declared that she lived on half of it and saved the other half—"

"For Margy!" declaimed Rose dramatically.

Helen drew her gaze back from the distance to smile quizzically at her younger sister.

"Perhaps!" she replied. "Who knows?"

"No one, yet. But Margy Blythe intends to soon, or know the reason why!" Margy folded up the letter and put it decisively back in the envelope. She got up quickly and Rose put out a hand as though to stop her.

"Where are you going?" she asked.

"To write J. Jones, Attorney, of course," retorted Margy. "About my inheritance, you know!" she added importantly, and left the room amidst a chorus of chuckles.

While she was gone Helen and Rose eagerly discussed the situation with their old friend, Miss Jessica Jellicoe.

"Wouldn't it be wonderful if Margy really did get some money out of this?" chuckled Rose. "Just like a fairy story or something!"

Little Miss Jellicoe nodded gravely.

"It would be very fine, my dear," she said. "But," with a dubious shake of the head, "as my dear mother said, 'tis neither safe nor wise to count your chickens before they're hatched.''

Although the girls appreciated the logic of this warning, they could no more help speculating about the letter of J. Jones, Attorney, and its import than they could have helped breathing. Had not the lawyer asserted that if Margy sent him her present address he would, in turn, favor her with an important communication?

Important communication! How many times following Miss Jessica Jellicoe's unexpected call at the uptown flat, that mysterious and delightful phrase fell from their tongues. How they turned it round and about and inside out in a vain effort to guess at its real meaning!

However, as they could not hope to receive word from J. Jones of Pogartown for at least a week, they were forced to content themselves with imaginings and wait for the eventful day when the ''important communication'' should arrive.

They had urged their kindly neighbor from Riverdale to stay with them for an indefinite visit, but the old lady gently but firmly refused on the ground that she was urgently needed at home. She did stay overnight with them, however, and long after she had left the city they looked back to that short visit as one of the bright spots in their workaday regime.

Not that life was in any way dull for the Blythe sisters—not at all! They had the happy gift of finding something to amuse and divert them in the simplest occurrence, bringing a cheerful spirit to their work that was almost more important than the work itself, and playing with an equal fervor and enthusiasm.

Down at the Lossar-Martin department store, Rose found her chums in the millinery trimmings department, where she herself worked, cordially interested in her account of the mysterious letter of J. Jones, Attorney, and the hint of an inheritance left by Aunt Margy Blythe to her namesake.

Annabelle Black stared at Rose, hands on hips, black eyes kindling with interest. Annabelle admirably fitted the last half of her name by reason of the fact that her hair and eyes were black, as well as her rather thick and bushy eyebrows. She was good looking, though, in a large-featured, striking manner and possessed a cheerful, though slightly domineering temperament. She was slangy and loud-spoken and, sometimes, almost offensively self-assertive, but her genuine kindness of heart made up to her friends for a great many faults.

Annabelle had been Rose's first friend in the store and had stood by her loyally through all sorts of difficulties. Rose was not the one to forget that sort of thing, and so the friendship between the two girls had steadily strengthened.

Rose's only other close friend in the depart-

ment was Roberta North, commonly known as
"Birdie" among her associates. This girl was
the exact antithesis of Annabelle Black. Shy,
hard-working, self-effacive, one would hardly
have known she was in the place, despite her almost ceaseless activity. Rose had often declared that Birdie did as much as any three of
the other girls, herself included, and never received any credit for it.

There had been once when her diligence was
rewarded, though Rose was the direct cause of
it, not Birdie. It had been Rose who had called
Mr. Beadle's attention to the fact that Birdie
North had become practically indispensable to
the millinery trimmings department.

The assistant manager had listened atten-
tively to Rose's recital of her friend's good
qualities, pronounced himself convinced, and,
accordingly, raised the girl's salary. As Birdie
had an invalid mother to support, this addition
to her small and inadequate income had been
a god-send and her former affection for Rose
changed to adoration. Rose had received an
increase at the same time, which had not been
unwelcome to her.

Since Herbert Shomberg, former floorwalker
in Rose's department, had been convicted of
stealing valuable merchandise from the Lossar-Martin store—for which crime Rose herself had been under suspicion for a consider-

able period—a strange peace had settled down over the department.

No new floorwalker had as yet been appointed. Miss O'Brien, department head, had been acting in a dual capacity. However, the girls were expecting daily to have a new despot appear, and curiosity was naturally high as to the type of man who would step into the shoes of Herbert Shomberg.

On this day, just before Rose imparted her information concerning Margy's queer inheritance, Annabelle Black contributed her own bit to the day's interest by declaring that the new floorwalker, a man named Henry Goos, was to take office that morning.

"If he turns out to be as bad as Mr. Shomberg, I'll hand in my resignation in a hurry," said Birdie North, smoothing back her mousecolored hair with a weary gesture. "I don't think I could stand having another one like him barking at me all day long."

"Cheer up, Birdie," Rose retorted. "They don't come as bad as Herbert Shomberg. This Goos man will have to be an improvement, no matter how mean he may be."

How she was to recall that observation before the end of the week and marvel at her ignorance!

Henry Goos!

About ten o'clock he was seen conferring earnestly with Miss O'Brien only a few coun-

ters away from the millinery trimmings. Being grateful for this opportunity of observing
their new chief unobserved, the girls availed
themselves of it.

Henry Goos was a man in his late forties,
tall, thin, long-featured. His eyes were sharp
and a trifle close together. His mouth, wide
and thin-lipped, drooped unpleasantly at the
corners, and, as though to match this droop, his
nose turned sharply inward at the tip, giving
to his whole face a sardonic, almost sinister expression.

"A likely-looking bird he is!" snorted Annabelle disgustedly though it may be noted that
she was very careful to lower her voice. "Looks
like one of them—what do you call the animal
that kills chickens and eats them? Oh, I know.
A hawk. That's what he is—a hawk."

"And we're the chickens," giggled Rose
nervously.

Annabelle gave her a worldly-wise stare and
nodded gravely.

"Right you are, Rose. You never spoke a
truer word."

"Maybe he isn't as bad as he looks," suggested Birdie, whose instinct it was to believe
the best of every one. "You can't always judge
by appearances, you know."

Annabelle, the aggressive, turned upon timid
Birdie North a look of mingled scorn and pity.

"Say, girlie, I'm willing to lay a hundred to

one bet right now that the way that bird looks
is nothing to the way he feels inside! I never
saw a mouth like that that wasn't a sure sign
of meanness. If I'm not much mistaken, we're
in for a sweet time with little Henry Goos!"

"Sh—get busy!" commanded Rose sharply.
"Here he comes!"

CHAPTER VI

A TREAT

As a matter of fact, Henry Goos, the new floorwalker, had left Miss O'Brien and was bearing down upon the millinery trimmings department like a "torpedo shot from a submarine." The comparison was Annabelle's. And it seemed from the look in his eyes that his murderous intent was the same.

He came straight up to Rose who, with Birdie and Annabelle, was ostentatiously and absorbedly arranging stock. He spoke in a high, irritable voice that the girls were to know very well in the days to come.

"I was watching you while I pretended to be absorbed in conversation with Miss O'Brien." he said, bending a severe gaze upon the astonished Rose. "You also were engaged in conversation, in company with your companions here," with a wave of the hand that included Birdie and Annabelle, "which, I may remind you, is not what the Lossar-Martin store is paying you for. In the future, you will, if you please, attend strictly to business."

"You old dried prune!" muttered Annabelle under her breath, watching the stiff back of Mr. Henry Goos as he stalked off in the direction of the east wing. "Of all the dried-up old crabs—"

"Hush—Miss O'Brien is watching you!" warned Rose, without turning her eyes in Annabelle's direction. "She is up to her old tricks again!"

Under the double watchfulness of Miss O'Brien and the new floorwalker, the girls exchanged scarcely a word until the lunch hour, when Rose and Birdie had planned to take their midday refreshment together. They turned about in this way, always leaving one girl to attend to the counter until the other two returned. There were exceptions to this rule, of course, the exceptions being bargain days and holiday times, when the girls went singly, snatched a few hurried mouthfuls of lunch and returned as quickly as possible to the counter.

On ordinary days, however, the former arrangement was very satisfactory, as customers were generally few and far between at the lunch hour and could be easily attended to by one girl.

Now, however, when Birdie and Rose repaired to the locker room to don hats and wraps they found themselves suddenly confronted by the steely-eyed Mr. Goos.

"Where are you going?" inquired the man sharply.

Rose bridled at the tone but managed to answer quietly enough.

"We were going to lunch," she said. "It is after twelve o'clock."

"You were going together?" asked the floor-walker.

Rose nodded, not trusting herself to answer this time. Birdie, she knew, was quivering with fright.

"That is absolutely against my rules," snapped the high-pitched voice. "The employees under my charge will go to lunch one at a time or not at all. I wish that to be understood now. You may go to lunch," he said to Birdie. "You may go back to the counter." This to Rose.

Her face flaming with indignation, Rose turned and, under the furtive scrutiny of girls at near-by counters, turned and walked back to the counter.

Birdie North looked after her chum, turned to Mr. Goos as though to utter a feeble protest, then fled abruptly toward the locker room.

Annabelle, burning with curiosity, since she had witnessed the whole thing from her place at the counter, did not dare even to question her chum.

Mr. Henry Goos seemed to be all over the store at once. Whatever one did, wherever one turned, one was sure to meet his steely gaze.

Miss O'Brien, who had been slightly shaken in her iron rule by the defection of the former floorwalker, had, with the aid of this new ally, regained all her former self-confidence and seemed bent upon making up for past laxity by an excess of severity toward the girls under her charge.

Feeling themselves constantly spied upon by these two superiors, the girls became self-conscious and nervous and committed mistakes and blunders that would ordinarily have been impossible.

It is safe to say that not one of the girls in the department of Henry Goos but what suffered one criticism on that eventful day. Some of them were reprimanded several times.

The day was unbearably hot and by the time five o'clock and release had rolled around, the girls were thoroughly worn out and disgusted.

"Meet me outside later," Annabelle said in an undertone to Rose, as they carefully prepared the counter for the night. "I've got to get this thing off my chest! Pass the good word on to Birdie."

The latter was apprised of the proposed indignation meeting and nodded wearily. Birdie always seemed to wilt more beneath the weight of conflict and trouble than did the other, more robust, girls. Birdie was not strong physically, and the mental burden of pity for her invalid mother and worry for fear she would not be

able to give the beloved invalid the care and
attention she so sorely needed, had sadly sapped
the frail girl's strength.

But no thought of giving up, of crying out
that the burden was too heavy for her slight
shoulders, had ever entered Birdie's mind.
When fortune smiled, as he so rarely did, she
was humbly grateful. When things went wrong,
as they so often did, she merely gritted her
teeth and worked more doggedly. And through
it all, Birdie never failed to summon up a smile
when she entered the tiny, hot apartment where
her mother spent such lonely days. Small wonder then, that warm-hearted, impulsive Rose
had grown to admire and love the quiet girl
and her sweet, patient mother. The troubles
of the North family were her troubles, their
small pleasures hers, as well.

The small increase in Birdie's salary had
done a great deal toward brightening the drab
life of this gallant mother and daughter. But
the interest of Rose Blythe and her frequent
visits to the invalid had accomplished more
than the money. Mrs. North had grown to love
her daughter's pretty friend very dearly, and
Rose returned the affection with all the impulsive warmth of her nature.

So now, at the end of this gruelling day,
Rose regarded her chum's white, haggard face
with real anxiety. She knew by the look in

Birdie's eyes that she was keeping on her feet by sheer effort of will.

They finished preparing the counter for the night and retired to the comparative freedom and privacy of the locker room. There Rose drew Annabelle Black's attention to Birdie's condition.

"She looks about ready to faint," said Rose in a whisper, lest Birdie overhear. "Some of these days she will just go to pieces altogether."

"Poor kid!" said Annabelle, her black eyes softening. "She sure does look about ready to kick the bucket. Needs a rest—a good long one."

"Looks as if she's likely to get it with our dear Henry Goos on the trail!" said Rose scornfully.

The conversation stopped abruptly as Birdie herself came up to them. Her cheap hat was drawn far down on her head, all but hiding the mouse-colored hair, and her face looked so small and pinched that Rose was startled anew.

"Let's get out of here—quick," she said abruptly. "There may be more air outside than there is in here, though, I must say, I doubt it!"

She put an arm about Birdie as they started toward the elevators and saw that she was trembling and that she staggered a little, as though dizzy or faint. Over the cheap little hat Annabelle and Rose exchanged anxious glances.

It was Annabelle Black, aggressive as usual, who opened the conversation as they reached the street.

"We've got to get Birdie to a restaurant and dose her with a sandwich and a chocolate soda." she proclaimed. "After which you can hear me rave about our new friend and jailor, Henry Goos. I'm going to keep it up for a couple of hours, at least—so get ready!"

But Birdie protested.

"I must get home right away," she said, raising a hand to her aching head. "Mother will worry—"

Rose had been studying her friend intently.

"Birdie North, how long is it since you tasted a good rare beefsteak?"

Birdie reddened, but spoke with a pitiful defiance.

"You know as well as I do, Posie, that mother has to have the beefsteak—if there is any. You know the doctor said she must have nourishing food."

"Great Scott, am I dreaming?" Annabelle Black was staring hard at Birdie, her black eyes round with incredulity. "Are you trying to tell me, Rose Blythe, that this crazy kid here starves herself?"

"I don't starve myself," declared Birdie, almost sullenly. "I get all I want to eat."

"Tell that to the marines, dearie," retorted

Annabelle in her usual atrocious slang. "I'll
say you couldn't prove it by your looks."

"Can't you come home with me, Birdie?
We'll make Annabelle come too and after din-
ner we will have a regular party calling Henry
Goos names."

Birdie shook her head.

"I can't leave mother," she repeated dully.
"I must go home."

"Say, this thing is as simple as the nose on
your face," cried Annabelle, in such loud and
joyful accents that several passers-by turned
to look at her inquiringly. "If Birdie has to go
home, we'll go too—only we will go armed. I
was the prize nut not to think of it before!
Come on, girls, make it snappy!"

They followed the aggressive one into a
butcher shop, Rose interested and expectant,
Birdie faintly protesting.

Annabelle purchased a steak large enough to
feed a family of six and then announced herself ready for a visit to a grocery store.

"There's a nice place not far from where we
live, and we'll not need to carry the things so
far," said Birdie, beginning to take more interest in the proceedings. "They have such wonderful asparagus. I've looked at it every day
coming home from work, but they want so
much for it—"

"Asparagus it is then," pronounced Annabelle, now thoroughly enjoying herself. She

had never before consciously set about the business of making some one else happy, and she was finding, to her surprise, that the experience was not unpleasant.

Annabelle had never seen Birdie's mother, although she had heard a great deal about the invalid from Rose. The aggressive and excitement-loving Annabelle had declared on several occasions that the sight of sickness or suffering made her "as blue as a robin's egg," and for that reason she seldom went out of her way to witness it.

Now she was amazed to find that she really looked forward to meeting Mrs. North. As for Birdie—it would be a treat for the eye to see that poor, white, drooping little thing devouring beefsteak and asparagus. All she could eat, for once!

They had a great time picking out the asparagus, and Rose insisted upon treating to cake and ice-cream from the little confectioner's shop around the corner from Birdie's flat.

From a drug store she telephoned to Hugh Draper's mother, who lived downstairs in their apartment house, and asked her to tell Helen that she would not be home until later and not to wait dinner for her.

By the time the girls reached the North flat, laden with bundles, Rose and Annabelle were in high good spirits. Only Birdie still drooped wearily and seemed to make her way up the steep dark stairs with difficulty. When they finally reached the door and she fumbled in her bag for the key the girl swayed dizzily, and again Rose put an anxious arm about her.

"Maybe I can find the key, dear, if you will let me look," she suggested, but at the moment Birdie drew forth the desired object and handed it to her.

"Open the door, please, Posie. I feel as though—I—oh—"

She half turned about, staggered dizzily, and would have toppled head first down the steep and narrow stairway had not Annabelle dropped her bundles and clutched wildly at her.

Her arms about the limp form of Birdie North, Annabelle stared amazedly at Rose.

"Great Scott, if she hasn't gone and fainted! Now, what do you know about that!"

CHAPTER VII

PLAY ACTING

FOR a moment Annabelle Black and Rose Blythe stared at each other in the dimness of the hall. Despite Annabelle's reputation for aggressiveness, it was Rose who first recovered her presence of mind.

"Don't let Mrs. North know if you can help it," Rose whispered, as she fitted the key in the lock with trembling fingers. "We will put Birdie on the couch in the front room—oh, why won't this door open?"

"Turn the key the other way—maybe it will work," suggested Annabelle, still holding Birdie's limp form. "And make it snappy, girlie. This kid isn't a heavy-weight, but then neither am I a strong man. One side, Posie, and give me a chance."

"Wait a minute. There, I've got it now. Remember," as the door swung inward, "don't tell Mrs. North. I'll make up some sort of story until we pull Birdie around again. Wait here till I put these bundles down," she added. "And I will help you carry her."

52

She slipped noiselessly into the apartment, fearful every moment that Mrs. North would call to her, deposited her bundles and ran back to Annabelle.

Together they managed to get Birdie into the living room and propped her up on the couch. At sight of the gray-white face, Rose felt a little faint herself. She rallied swiftly and gave directions to Annabelle in a cautious undertone.

"The kitchen is over there," she said, nodding toward the rear of the small room they were in. "Get water and bathe her face quickly, Annabelle. She looks as if she were—dead. I'll go and tell Mrs. North that Birdie is coming in a minute."

Annabelle nodded curtly, her natural aggressiveness rebelling at this flood of admonition.

"Sure, you go fix it with the old lady. I'll 'tend to Birdie here."

Rose nodded and returned swiftly to the front door. There she got the bundles that Annabelle had dropped in order to catch Birdie. She put these quickly on the table in the living room, then returned once more to the door.

She made a great fuss with the key in the lock as though she were opening the door all over again, then called out cheerily to Mrs. North.

The latter answered gladly from the little

room at the rear of the hall that was her prison
day after day, month after month, year after
year. The eagerness in that welcoming voice
made Rose's heart ache, it spoke so elo-
quently of the invalid's loneliness.

The girl hurried to the door, opened it
quickly and, as quickly, slipped inside the
room. Mrs. North held out both hands to her
and Rose bent down and kissed her cheek.

"I had a feeling you would come to-night,"
Birdie's mother said, patting the girl's hand
in her withered one. "It seems so long since
I have seen you, dear, though it is really only
a week—a week of endless days, one just like
the other." This was the nearest Rose had
ever heard the invalid come to complaining and
as though she regretted instantly that she had
spoken so, Mrs. North added quickly: "But
where is Birdie? She must have come in with
you."

"She stopped to buy something at the store.
She'll be here in just a minute," said Rose,
her face flushing with embarrassment as she
uttered the little subterfuge. "She did stop
too. We all did!" she told herself fiercely.
"And what do you think?" she added aloud
and gayly, to disguise the fact that she was
close to tears: "You and Birdie are going to
have two guests to dinner to-night—your
respected young friend, Rose Blythe, and
another girl from the store."

"That's nice," said Mrs. North, her thin, sweet face lighting with a quick interest. "Where is this girl?"

"She is with Birdie," answered Rose. "They will both be in in a moment." That was the truth, thought Rose gratefully.

As soon as she could, she made an excuse to get away into the living room. There she found Birdie trying to sit up and Annabelle resolutely holding her down.

"Now don't be any more foolish than you can help, Birdie North," the latter was adjuring, impatiently. "Can't you stop struggling and worrying for half a second and just lie still and rest?"

"But—mother—she musn't know!" muttered Birdie, redoubling her struggle to sit up. "If she had to worry about me, she just couldn't get on at all!"

Rose gently pushed Annabelle aside and put an arm behind Birdie's shoulders, helping her to a sitting posture.

"There, there, don't worry, honey," she whispered soothingly. "Your mother doesn't know you are sick and she won't have to, if you will just try to pull yourself together."

Birdie clung to her friend and the tears of weakness welled to her eyes.

"I might have known you would take care of her Posie," she muttered. "What did you tell her?"

"That you had stopped to get something at the store and would be in in a minute," answered Rose, smoothing back the girl's disordered hair. "Now if you can just pull yourself together—"

"Yes—yes! I'm all right now!" Birdie pulled her blouse together at the throat and smiled faintly. "Give me a little powder, Posie and maybe she won't notice—"

"Here, use mine," Annabelle broke in, producing from some mysterious receptacle a complete vanity case. "The man who sold it to me said it would cover up anything and everything and was guaranteed to make any one beautiful."

"Well, if it does that to me, it will be going some!" remarked Birdie ruefully, patting powder on her shiny nose and doing her utmost to remove the traces of her faintness. Her face was still shockingly white and her lips were a peculiar bluish gray. She got unsteadily to her feet. Rose put a supporting arm about her while Annabelle restored the vanity case to its mysterious hiding place.

As they reached the door to her mother's room, Birdie straightened up and gently shook off Rose's arm.

"I'm all right, Posie," she said, took a long breath, and flung open the door.

Immediately there was a transformation. She was no longer the pallid, frail girl they had seen but a moment before, but a cheerful, happy young person to whom the hard day's work at the store was only a pleasant game.

Annabelle watched with astonishment this girl she had thought she knew so well and whom she really knew so little. To the best of her ability she acknowledged Birdie's gay introduction of her to her mother. But there were tears in her sharp black eyes as she turned back into the kitchen with Rose.

"Say, that girl in there is some play actor," she confided to the latter, in a husky whisper. "Listen to her chatter, will you? You wouldn't believe that just a minute ago she was dead to the world. Now I ask you, am I right or wrong? What are you going to do?" she asked curiously as Rose ran into the other room and returned with some of the packages they had brought.

"I'm going to broil this steak," said Rose, adding with a break in her voice: "Do you know what's the matter with that girl? She's just starving herself to death!"

CHAPTER VIII

J. Jones, Again

When Birdie North returned to the kitchen the girls pushed her into a chair and insisted upon getting the meal themselves.

Mrs. North was wheeled into the kitchen too, and placed in the coolest corner of it to watch operations.

"Though you are to have nothing to say about the cooking," Rose told her gayly. "Annabelle and I are very touchy. We won't be dictated to. Oh-h-h—"

"What's the matter now?" asked Annabelle, while Birdie half started from her chair in alarm.

"The ice-cream!" wailed Rose. "I forgot all about it and I venture to say it's soup."

"Ice-cream!" exclaimed Mrs. North happily. "Well, this is a real party!"

"Maybe you won't think so, when you see it. The ice-cream, I mean—not the party," warned Rose.

However, the ice-cream, though softened considerably by its sojourn in the heat of the

living room, was not in an entirely hopeless
state.

"If you will put it right on top of the ice
it ought to harden by the time we get ready
for it," said Birdie. She rose as though to
follow her own advice, but Annabelle pushea
her unceremoniously back into her chair.

"Take my advice, girlie, and rest yourself
while you can," she said. Then, noting the
anxious look Mrs. North turned upon Birdie,
she tried clumsily to make up for the blunder.
"You work harder than any two of us at the
store. Now it's our turn."

Annabelle was rewarded by a grateful glance
from Birdie and a relieved sigh from the
invalid. Rose guessed in that moment that
Mrs. North knew her daughter was far from
strong, despite Birdie's gallant efforts to keep
such knowledge from her and was constantly
worried and anxious about her. The pitiful
thing was that there was no escape for either
of them. Mrs. North was helpless because of
her invalidism. Birdie must work unceasingly
for the pittance she earned at the store, unable
to rest or turn aside, going on and on, until,
some day, perhaps, she would drop in the
harness. Then what would become of her—of
her mother?

"Oh, if I only had a million dollars!"
thought Rose longingly, the while she cut the
bread and put the butter on the table. "Just

make believe I wouldn't know what to do with it!''

But they had the merriest kind of supper for all that. Rose and Annabelle, inexperienced as they were in culinary work, managed to turn out one of the juciest, tenderest steaks ever broiled and a huge dish of asparagus with drawn butter sauce that would have done credit to any French chef in existence.

Mrs. North's cheeks grew bright under the stimulus of the young folks chatter and the excellent food. As for Birdie—well, the change in her was marvelous. She ate her portion of steak with an appetite she could not disguise and consumed the asparagus so eagerly that Rose felt a sort of rage surge up in her heart. Something was all wrong somewhere, when a girl like Birdie North was forced to regard ordinary things like beefsteak and asparagus as luxuries.

Then she thought, with a sort of panic that, not so long ago she and her sisters had been as badly off as Birdie North. There had been a time when they had faced actual want, had been forced to leave the house in the morning, hungry. Oh, yes, she knew just what it was!

After they had finished the ice-cream and cake everything seemed to take on a rosier hue. Even the advent of Mr. Henry Goos, the new floorwalker, seemed less important than it had during the day.

"Maybe he's just all swelled up with his own importance," said Annabelle, picking up the last scrap of sponge cake and munching on it contentedly. "Perhaps after Goosey has been on the job for a few days longer, he'll come down off his high horse and be human. Snappy old hawk. I'd like to give him an idea of what the girls think of him. Maybe he wouldn't be so fresh."

After a while the talk drifted around to Rose's tale of the communication sent to Margy from J. Jones, Attorney, of Pogartown.

"I should think you would be dreadfully excited. I know I'd be," said Birdie, her eyes wide with interest. "Maybe the old lady was really rich and has left Margy all her money."

"Humph!" snorted Annabelle, skeptically. "Probably left her her pet puppy and a canary bird. If I was you, dearie, I wouldn't lie awake nights worrying about the million!"

"Which reminds me," said Rose, getting up briskly, "that if I don't get back pretty soon, Helen will have the police reserves out after me. Come on, Annabelle, let's wash the dishes and go home."

In spite of Birdie's protests, the girls cleaned up thoroughly and not till the last pan was carefully put away would they think of leaving.

Rose kissed Mrs. North with more than usual affection when she said good-bye and the hands of the invalid clung to hers as though she were reluctant to let her go at all.

Birdie, following the girls to the door and trying to thank them for their kindness, choked up and could not say a word. Rose put an arm about her, whispering words of encouragement. Then, feeling in a curious way that she was deserting two people who needed her very much, she turned and followed Annabelle down the dark and narrow stairs.

The two girls spoke very little on the way uptown. As she neared her station Annabelle broke the rather long silence between them.

"No use talking, Posie, something's got to be done for that girl. Poor kid. Why, I never had an idea she was so game. She sort of made me ashamed of myself for complaining about anything. But if somebody doesn't come to her rescue—and that pretty soon too—she and her poor mother are going to be on the rocks. Gee, I can't help wishing I was your sister Margy with a chance of grabbing that million!"

Rose smiled rather wryly.

"If Birdie's chance of help depended on that million, I'd feel sorrier for her than I do!" she said.

On the rest of that uptown ride, after Annabelle had left her, Rose still thought moodily of Birdie. If Henry Goos continued his present method of espionage and adverse criticism, the burden of work at the Lossar-Martin department store would be greatly increased—that much was certain. And how was poor Birdie North to bear any extra pressure, she who was already so over-burdened?

"Oh, why, why did they put such a man in that position?" cried Rose. "We just can't help having trouble with him. I almost dread to go down to the store in the morning."

Henry Goos did not improve as the days went by, and the girls began to feel at last that they were indeed in prison with a ruthless jailor in the guise of the new floorwalker.

While Rose was having her troubles at the store, Margy and Helen were very busy too, each in her particular line of work.

Margy was getting along famously with her eccentric employer, Miss Dorcas Pepper. Her night school work she found so interesting that she became more and more fixed in her determination to let nothing interfere with her business career.

Lloyd Roberts, whom she had met through Joe Morris, a friend of Rose's, was attentive —and would have been much more so, had Margy given him the slightest encouragement.

Margy received candy and flowers from Lloyd Roberts and went with him to an occasional show or dance, but she was always indifferent to his attentions, and sometimes he even seemed to bore her a little.

In this she was different from her other two

sisters. Helen and Rose thoroughly enjoyed the society of the men who called upon them, and loved the fun and excitement that these young people gave them.

Hugh Draper, a young lawyer living in the apartment below the Blythes, had been strongly attracted by the dreamy, talented Helen. Since Helen returned the liking, the two had become firm friends.

Joe Morris, office manager of the Reynolds Moving Company, had been responsible for many of the good times shown the girls and was a special friend of golden-haired, vivid Rose. Since Joe Morris had been influential in fastening suspicion upon Herbert Shomberg, the dishonest floorwalker at the Lossar-Martin department store and so removing suspicion from Rose, the two had been better friends than ever.

Dale Elton, the young newspaper reporter who had befriended Margy in the park, had called to see Margy at the apartment and, finding her not at home, had spent a very pleasant evening with Helen and Rose. Then an assignment for his paper called him to a distant city and the girls promptly forgot his existence.

They had other things—far more important things—to think about!

Rose was surprised one afternoon on leaving the Lossar-Martin store in the company of

Birdie and Annabelle, to find her two sisters waiting for her.

"You perfect peaches!" she cried, flinging her arms about them and hugging them, regardless of the interested stares of passers-by. "What a joyful surprise! Has anything special happened?"

"We have heard from J. Jones of Pogartown!" cried Helen and Margy breathlessly and together.

CHAPTER IX

A Small Fortune

"Oh-h!" cried Rose, recklessly blocking traffic in the crowded street and blissfully unaware of it. "The inheritance! Margy! Helen! Tell me quick! What is it?"

"We don't know ourselves yet," replied Helen, as Margy seized the younger girl by the arm and drew her toward the plateglass window of the store where she would be out of the way of the hurrying crowds. Annabelle and Birdie followed, looking on eagerly.

"Don't know yet!" gasped Rose. "Do you mean to stand there and tell me you haven't opened the letter?"

"Letters, you should say," corrected Margy, enjoying her sister's excitement and mystification. "J. Jones, Attorney, was very generous. He wrote us a letter apiece."

"Then give me mine quickly before I go crazy!" demanded Rose, her cheeks flushed to match her name, her eyes bright. "Margy Blythe, how can you be so exasperating!"

But Margy only shook her head.

"We aren't going to open anything until we get home where we can swoon, if we feel like it," she said determinedly. "Helen and I waited to get you so that you could be in on the party, and now you can wait a little while too."

"Then let's get home quick. You girls may have the patience of Job, but I'm quite sure I haven't!"

Rose had seized her two sisters by the arm and was actually propelling them down the street before she recalled the presence of Annabelle and Birdie.

She paused penitently and turned to them.

"Can't you come, too?" she asked. "We could get a bite of dinner and then open the letters together."

The girls were strongly tempted, but were finally forced to refuse the alluring invitation.

"I've got a date with a boy who gets sore every time I turn him down," Annabelle told them airily. "I've done it twice already, and I don't dare do it again if I value some future good times. So long! You can count on us to listen to all you have to tell in the morning, Posie."

"Mother will be expecting me," said Birdie wistfully. "Good-bye, dear, and good luck."

Rose waved to them and then marched her sisters rapidly toward the subway.

"I say, hold on a bit, will you, my child?"

protested Margy, as she and Helen found themselves piloted across the busy street with a speed and recklessness that very nearly precipitated them beneath the wheels of a swiftly moving auto truck. "We don't have to catch a train, you know, and this is a hot, hot day. Also, I have no great ambition to have my name on the casualty list to-morrow morning."

"You'll find mine heading it, if you don't hurry," warned Rose. "I tell you, I feel myself weakening rapidly. I can stand this suspense but a short time longer."

On the interminable ride uptown in the subway she thought to ask them how it was that they had been waiting together at the Lossar-Martin store for her.

"You were at Miss Pepper's to-day?" she asked of Margy.

The latter nodded.

"It was Nell who brought the joyful news to me," she explained. "The letters came to the house this afternoon—but you tell her about it, Nell."

"As soon as the postman handed me the three business-looking envelopes, I felt sure they were from J. Jones," complied Helen, raising her voice to carry above the grinding roar of the subway. "Then when I saw the Pogartown postmark I knew for sure that we had word of the inheritance—"

"But how is it there were three envelopes?"
demanded Rose eagerly. "I thought Margy was
the one who was to get the inheritance."

"It seems we are in on it, too," replied
Helen. "Though I suppose if Aunt Margy has
left anything, the bulk of it goes to Margy here
because she was named after the old lady."

"Then you went straight to Miss Pepper's
to tell Margy," suggested Rose, eager for the
rest of the story. Helen shook her head.

"I thought I would wait till night on the
chance she would come up to the house after
school," she said. "Then I got to thinking
that she was just as likely to go back to Miss
Pepper's for the night, and I felt as if we simply
couldn't wait till to-morrow to know what was
in those letters—"

"I should say not!" cried Rose emphatically.
"I say, Margy, aren't you going to let me see
even the outside of the envelope?" she added
pleadingly.

"Ask Helen!" returned Margy. "I wouldn't
let her give me mine for fear I should open it
and spoil everything. We were bound to wait
for you, you see."

"And you are a pair of ducks to do it,"
Rose returned gratefully. "It would have
taken half the fun away if you had known ahead
of time."

Helen pulled an envelope from her bag and
held it out toward Rose.

"Here's yours," she said.

But Rose shook her head, closing her eyes tight against temptation.

"If you and Margy can wait, I guess I can," she said. "Put it back, Helen Blythe, before I grab it."

The long train ride was over at last and the girls fairly ran the short distance to their apartment. At the steps they very nearly ran down a good-looking, tall young man whose quizzical gray eyes regarded them laughingly.

"Where's the fire?" he wanted to know. "Let me help put it out."

"There isn't any fire, Hugh Draper, as you very well know," said Rose. "But we have a very good reason for being in a hurry, nevertheless."

"I say, what's all the mystery about?" protested Hugh, following the girls into the hall and addressing himself particularly to Helen. "There is something stirring. I can smell it!"

"That's corn beef and cabbage you smell from the second floor front," retorted the irrepressible Rose who, with Margy, was already half way up the stairs. When Helen would have followed, Hugh Draper put a detaining hand on her arm.

"I was hoping we could go out somewhere together to-night, Helen. Can't we?" he pleaded.

Helen hesitated. An evening with Hugh Draper was always pleasant, but this evening was a little different.

"I can't Hugh, not to-night," she said, adding quickly as disappointment clouded his face: "But if you will come up for a little while later in the evening, we may have something interesting to tell you."

"Will I come?" returned the young lawyer, with his pleasant laugh. "Would a duck swim?"

Helen quickly followed her sisters to find them pacing up and down impatiently in the small living room.

"You look like those Bengal tigers at the zoo," she laughed.

"Thanks very much!" retorted Rose, and made a spring for her.

"Give me my letter, Helen Blythe, before I die!" she demanded. "Come, now, stand and deliver!"

"But I thought we were going to wait till after dinner," Helen protested, and was interrupted by a howl of exasperation from Rose.

"Helen Blythe, are you made of stone?" she wailed. "Give me my mail at once or I shan't answer for the consequences!"

"Let's open them one at a time," Margy suggested. Then we can have three surprises. You first, Rose, then Helen; then mine."

Rose nodded and tore open the envelope.

Inside was a brief note from J. Jones, Attorney, stating that he inclosed to Miss Rose Blythe a Liberty Bond for a hundred dollars, her share of the inheritance of the estate left by Miss Margaret Blythe of Pogartown.

"A hundred dollars!" breathed Rose ecstatically drawing forth the Liberty Bond. "It means just about as much to me as a thousand would to most people. Now, Helen—yours!" she turned eagerly to her older sister.

Helen opened the envelope addressed to her to find that it contained a Liberty Bond of the same denomination as that bequeathed to Rose by their eccentric maiden aunt.

"Two hundred dollars!" cried Margy. "My, but the Blythe family is beginning to come up in the world!"

"But open yours, hurry, Marg!" commanded Rose. "Don't you suppose we have any curiosity at all?"

Margy took up the envelope addressed to her and fingered it gingerly.

"Well, here goes!" she cried, and tore open the flap.

CHAPTER X

On Board

HELEN and Rose crowded close to Margy on the couch and peered eagerly over her shoulder at the letter from J. Jones of Pogartown.

Breathless, they read it through together, then stared at each other. They were greatly mystified and rather disappointed. Not till that moment had they realized how much they had hoped that Margy might really inherit something of value from this eccentric relative of whom they knew so little.

"Furniture!" cried Rose from the depths of her disappointment. "Haircloth furniture and an old hall clock!"

"And a box of flour; don't forget that," Helen reminded her. "I suppose we ought to find the whole thing—amusing," she added.

"Amusing!" repeated Rose, in huge disgust. "Well, I'll tell you, I need something more than that to amuse me. I think it's a mean joke. That's what I think!"

"Oh, I don't know!" said Margy slowly. She had been studying the letter and now she looked up with a queer gleam in her eye.

"Did you read what she wants done with the flour?"

"No, and I don't intend to, either," said Rose crossly. A box of wheat flour was not a very romantic substitute for a million dollars, she thought.

"Then you missed something!" Margy retorted smartly. "I believe Aunt Margy had something in the back of her eccentric old head, only it pleased her humor to disguise the fact."

" 'Disguise' is the word," muttered Rose.

"Look here, Nell!" Margy took no notice of her younger sister. She motioned Helen to a seat beside her with increasing excitement. "There is something more here than meets the eye. Just read that!"

She pointed to a paragraph near the end of the letter and Helen bent over to read it carefully.

Drawn, despite herself, by curiosity, Rose slowly approached and also read the paragraph.

"Your aunt, Margaret Blythe, expressed an earnest wish that you, her niece and namesake, should bake all the flour in the box that will be expressed to you, into biscuits and bread—"

"I wonder what would happen if you made cake," suggested Rose, and for answer Margy pointed to the written page.

"Read, my child," she said solemnly.

"Your aunt stipulated that under no circumstances should the flour be used for baking cake—"

"Of all idiotic things!" cried Rose, but Margy motioned her to silence while she read the last sentence of the paragraph aloud.

"In the event that you carry out these instructions carefully, you will advise me of the fact, and, at such time, may hear further concerning your inheritance.
"Yours respectfully,
"J. JONES, *Attorney.*"

"Well, now, what do you know about that?" cried Rose. She sat down suddenly, realizing that her knees were weak. "Did you ever hear such nonsense?"

"What do you suppose it means?" asked Helen curiously. "Your inheritance certainly can't be in the flour tin. I don't see where all this bread making comes in."

"Oh, but that may be just it!" exclaimed Rose, with renewed excitement. "Maybe Aunt Margy hid her jewels in the flour and expects that every time you bake some bread or biscuits you will find some of them."

"Every time you break a tooth, you find a

diamond!'' chuckled Margy. ''I must say I wouldn't mind finding a few jewels in my daily bread, but at that I'm not particularly anxious for a set of false teeth.''

''Maybe you can suggest something more reasonable,'' said Rose.

Helen laughed.

''We couldn't suggest anything less reasonable,'' she said. ''A barrel of jewels wrapped in flour! Guess again, Rose.''

''Well, the whole thing is just about as unreasonable as anything I ever heard of.''

''And the haircloth furniture!'' cried Helen, looking helplessly about her. ''How on earth are we going to make room for it? We have too much furniture in here now.''

''We will have to put it on the roof, I guess, or sell it at auction,'' said Margy grimly. ''I must say, my inheritance hasn't given me great joy as yet.''

''J. Jones says it is on the way now,'' said Rose. ''Furniture, hall clock, flour box, and all.''

''That means that the days of my idleness are nearly at an end,'' said Margy, with a sigh. ''I shall soon have to start baking bread!''

''What I want to know,'' said Rose, with a teasing grin, ''is whether or not we shall be expected to eat it!''

''I warn you, woman, to get out of my way!''

cried Margy, in a sepulchral tone. "I am about to throw this pillow at you!"

Rose ducked nimbly and the missile went flying over her golden head.

"Missed me!" she jeered. "By a good foot, too. My, what a shot!"

They made a merry time of dinner that night and the more they thought of Aunt Margy's queer bequest, the more impressed they became with the mystery surrounding it.

Why should this old lady insist that Margy bake all the flour into bread and biscuits before she should learn anything further concerning her inheritance?

Of course the whole thing was odd, but the very queerness was its charm. They began to long with a sort of breathless interest for the day when Margy's extraordinary inheritance should arrive from Pogartown.

Hugh Draper came in later in the evening, bearing with him a brick of ice-cream and listened with a great deal of interest to their news.

"At least you have the two hundred dollars in Liberty Bonds," he said. "But I believe with Margy here that the old lady really has left something of value, money or property which it pleased her eccentric humor to disguise by this elaborate rigmarole.

"By jove," he added, with a grin, "I believe she has left Margy her house and wants to be sure she's a good housekeeper before she takes

over the duties. This sort of thing is enough
to make a fellow turn detective!''

"That's it!'' cried Rose delightedly. "Margy's in training to run a boarding house!''

"Not I!'' exclaimed Margy. "Oh, dear me!
that J. Jones knows, but I suppose he won't
tell until the very last speck of the old flour is
baked into bread! How can we wait, girls?''

For a little while after the receipt of the
communications from J. Jones, the girls could
think of little but the mystery of Margy's inheritance. But as the days went by and there
was no sign of furniture or flour box, they
turned their attention to other things. After
all, it would take considerable time for so much
crated stuff to travel from Pogartown, Iowa, to
New York, and there was no use, they decided,
just sitting around and waiting for it.

So, when Joe Morris suggested that they
make up a party for the following Saturday
afternoon and take the boat up the Hudson for
Bear Mountain, the girls readily fell in with the
idea.

The prospect of getting away from the heat
and din of the city even for so short a time was
extremely alluring to them, and they went
about their preparations with enthusiasm.

"Too bad Margy hasn't got her box of
flour,'' teased Rose. "She could bake us some
bread to take along!''

When Saturday afternoon and the boys—

Joe Morris, Hugh Draper, and Lloyd Roberts
—arrived, they found the girls and a huge box
of lunch waiting for them.

"Looks as if we have enough here to keep
off the wolf for a little while," grinned Joe
Morris, as he hefted the box. "We'll have to
take turns carrying the lunch, fellows. Give us
an appetite!"

Their good spirits persisted even through
the hot journey to the boat which was to bear
them up the Hudson. But when they were once
aboard and settled comfortably on deck the real
fun of the trip began.

"Oh, just smell that breeze!" cried Rose,
stretching her arms luxuriously toward the
glassy water. "There wasn't a breath of air
stirring in the city."

"You just wait till we get going," Joe Morris
promised. "You'll find more than a breath of
air stirring then."

"Here we go!" cried Margy, as the boat
quivered and moved slowly out from the dock.
"I'm going up forward where I can see everything."

"You will blow away, if you do," Helen
warned her. "Better stay here."

But Margy shook her head and proceeded
forward, Lloyd Roberts at her elbow, steering
a clever course between deck chairs and the
crowds that thronged the deck.

There they sat, reveling in the breeze that

swept them refreshingly. Finally the others, fired by their example, joined them.

It was a glorious sail with new, fairylike vistas opening up at every turn and bend in the magic, winding river.

"Oh, it is too lovely!" cried Helen, her eyes misty with delight. "Hugh—oh, Hugh—I wish I had brought my brushes and canvas with me. Look at that little miniature island with the mountain towering in the background and the water, like silver, gleaming all about it. I will paint that picture, Hugh." She closed her eyes as though to impress the beauty of the scene upon her mind. "I will sketch it in from memory and call it the 'Isle of Dreams.'"

Hugh Draper watched her, his gray eyes soft.

"You are a wonderful girl, Helen, and I know that will be a wonderful picture. Some day, I will be able to say, 'I knew her, when—!'" he added whimsically.

Helen flushed with pleasure and shook her head with a little deprecating gesture.

"I have not done much yet," she said. "I have only wanted to!"

It seemed a very short time to them before they reached Bear Mountain. In company with their fellow excursionists, they gathered up various picnic paraphernalia in preparation for the landing.

They stepped from the boat, tramped up the long hill to the public grounds, and then, after a look around, followed Joe Morris towards the woods.

"We must find a nice spot for lunching," said Margy.

They wandered on through the woods, gradually leaving their fellow passengers behind while they hunted for an appropriate spot to picnic in.

"Three whole hours before the boat starts back," said Rose happily. "I could stay here for ten."

"Good gracious!" exclaimed Margy, as Lloyd Roberts helped her over a huge bowlder in the path. "I felt a drop. It is going to rain!"

CHAPTER XI

THE CAVE

"RAIN!" cried the others incredulously, staring up at a sky which, but a moment before, had been a beautiful turquoise blue.

"You must be—" began Rose, but stopped abruptly as she saw that the sky was no longer blue but heavily overcast with dark and lowering clouds.

At the same time Helen felt a drop of rain against her cheek. Then came another, and another.

"Say, wouldn't that make you tired!" cried Joe Morris disconsolately. "Not a drop of rain for a week and now—the deluge."

"Better get somewhere under cover, and pretty quick, too," suggested Hugh. "If I am not much mistaken, that is thunder I hear rumbling in the distance."

"You are not mistaken!" said Lloyd Roberts grumpily. "But the question now before the house is, where do we go from here?"

"We might get back to the pavilion on the mountain top above the landing," suggested Helen, but Hugh shook his head.

"The storm would beat us to it," he said. "Better find some sort of shelter in the neighborhood, if we can."

This "if" seemed a big one. Although they scurried around for several minutes in a vain effort to find shelter, there seemed to be nothing in the vicinity capable of furnishing greater protection than the trees.

Although the girls had huddled under a group of these forest monarchs to escape the now steadily falling rain, they soon abandoned even this poor shelter. The growling of the thunder became louder, more ominous, and the lightning cut in sinister forked tongues across the sky.

The trees had become a menace, attracting the lightning.

The boys, who had been searching more eagerly than ever for shelter, came back to the girls, reluctantly announcing failure.

"Guess we'll have to make a break for the pavilion, after all," said Hugh. "Nothing to be gained by hanging around here. That's a sure thing!"

They started back on the run, but the storm was like some merciless giant, pursuing them, gaining on them ruthlessly.

The flash of the lightning blinded them, the thunder struck against the mountain, reverberating back upon them with a deafening crash.

A sudden, tremendous clap, the sound of rending and splintering, and a sudden wild scream from Helen.

"Rose! Look out! That tree! Look out!"

Joe Morris was the next to see the toppling tree, to sense the horrible peril of the girl who, running a few feet ahead of him, was directly in its path.

Without stopping to think, acting entirely on instinct, Joe leaped for her, struck her aside, flinging her forward on her face.

The tree, falling with hideous velocity was directly above him, the branches breaking and snapping like twigs in its fall.

He could hear the frantic shouts of his companions, fancied he could feel the crushing weight of the great tree upon him. Driven by the instinct of self-preservation, Joe put all his strength into one tremendous leap.

He sprawled upon the ground, digging his hands into the soft earth and behind him heard a tremendous thud.

For a moment he thought he had been struck and lay motionless, not daring to stir.

Rose was safe—thank fortune, Rose was safe!

In a daze he could see her sitting up, scrambling to her feet, coming toward him.

Other hands had reached him. He was being turned over, pulled to a sitting posture. His head had struck upon a stone in falling, and half dazed him. He drew a hand wonderingly across his brow.

Faces bent above him, white faces, anxious faces. Then a vigorous young person pushed them all aside and sank to her knees beside him.

"Joe! Joe Morris! you aren't hurt?" Rose demanded. "Oh, look, there is blood on his forehead! He has been hurt! Lend me your handkerchief somebody—quick!"

Several handkerchiefs were found and offered, but by the time Rose had torn one of them in strips Joe had recovered from his dizziness and was once more quite able to take care of himself.

"I'm all right," he protested, as Rose carefully wiped away the blood on his forehead and examined the wound anxiously. "It's only a scalp wound, Posie. Take more than that to kill me!"

"You—you needn't joke about it!" said Rose, and swallowed hard over a lump in her throat. "You—you saved my life, Joe Morris, whether you know it or not."

"And also knocked you face down in the dirt," returned Joe, with a dry smile. "Something tells me that wasn't any way to treat a lady!"

Somebody giggled, and the tension was over.

And, as the storm was far from subsiding and they were becoming drenched by the driving rain, Joe was helped to his feet by the two other young men and they continued on toward the boat landing.

The boys had already taken off their jackets and flung them about the shoulders of the girls to protect their light summer frocks, and now their clothes clung to them wetly, giving them a miserable, sodden appearance.

"Fine kind of holiday this is!" grumbled Hugh Draper, helping Helen with one hand and Joe with the other. "We might better have stayed on the boat."

"Oh, look, what's that?" cried Helen suddenly, and pointed to a dark, yawning hole in the mountainside.

"A cave!" cried Margy joyfully. "Oh, you blessed infant—you have actually discovered a cave!"

CHAPTER XII

A New Peril

'A concerted dash was made for the promised shelter of that hole in the side of the mountain. Even Joe seemed to regain his normal strength at the hope of shelter from the storm.

Rose was the first to poke her pretty head into the mouth of the cave, and Joe reached for her, drawing her back rather roughly.

"You don't know what's in that cave," he reminded her, as she looked at him, surprised. "It may be the home of some animal."

"A wildcat," giggled Rose, "Or, maybe, a bear."

"You never can tell," said Joe, with a grin and together the three young fellows entered the cave.

The place was dark and smelled rather damp and unpleasant, but, at that, it was not nearly so damp as the out-of-doors!

Having used the larger half of a box of matches in an attempt to solve the mystery of the cave, the boys finally decided that if any animals lived there, they were not home at the present time and turned back to invite the girls in.

They found the latter in the act of entering without any invitation.

"Did you suppose we were going to stay out there all day?" Rose asked them, her voice coming spookily through the darkness of the interior. "I would rather face a wild animal than that ferocious storm. Listen to that thunder!"

"It's immense!" cried Margy, who, as had her father, always gloried in electric storms. She declared it fired her imagination, made her feel like doing great things. "I wouldn't be surprised if the whole mountain went next."

"My, but you have a cheerful disposition," sighed Helen. "Do you realize that if the mountain goes, our cave goes with it—to say nothing of ourselves? What have you got in here?" she asked of the young men, as she gropingly felt her way along one wall of the cave."

"Nothing but a large amount of darkness and dankness so far," confessed Hugh. "We can't even invite you ladies to sit down," he added, with a chuckle.

"Seems to be a fairly big place," Margy commented, and for her benefit Lloyd Roberts struck another match.

The tiny, flickering flame lighted the place

cheerily. It fell also on something the boys had not seen in their first quick inspection of the place—something that resembled a coiled rope in a far corner of the cave.

They saw suddenly, and the girls as well, that it was not a rope, but something cold, sinister, something that lifted an ugly head, that writhed in hideous suggestion.

The match went out, burned down to the end in Lloyd's suddenly stiffened fingers. In a moment a hand was upon his arm, a voice hissed through the darkness:

"Keep still! Don't speak! Don't move!"

The girls obeyed automatically. As a matter of fact, it is doubtful whether, at that moment, they could have moved if they had tried.

Lloyd heard Hugh Draper's voice again in a swift, commanding whisper:

"Light another match! I'll do the rest!"

Lloyd Roberts fumbled for the matches, almost dropped the box, swiftly made a light.

The feeble flame fell again upon that cold, immobile object in the corner of the cave. Immobile for a moment only. In the feeble flare of the match, the reptile seemed again to recognize its enemies. Its flattened, ugly head drew back upon the neck as it prepared to strike.

Helen screamed, suddenly terrified.

"Hugh, jump!" she entreated frantically. "Get out of the way. Oh—h—" The cry

ended in a wail as the reptile uncoiled its sinister length and seemed to catapult through the
air!

The match again went out, leaving them in
a curtain of darkness that was rent by the terrified cries of the girls.

Hugh's voice came to them—calm, reassur-
ing.

"It's all right. I've got him. Light a
match, somebody."

But both Joe and Lloyd had already struck
a light and in its illumination they saw the
amazing tableau.

On the upward climb from the boat landing,
Hugh Draper had picked up a curious, forked
stick. In the crotch of this he had caught the
reptile when it struck, had caught it neatly and
squarely behind the flattened head, and pinned
it to the earth. There its uncoiled, sinister body
thrashed in impotent fury. The little eyes
gleamed angrily, the forked tongue darted furiously in and out, but it was helpless.

The girls stared, fascinated, unable to believe
their eyes. But Hugh's voice, cool and commanding, roused them again to the need of
action.

"Get out of here, girls," he ordered. "And
somebody get me a rock, half a dozen, if you
can find them. I don't know how long I shall
be able to hold this boy. He is a pretty slippery
customer."

There was a rush for the mouth of the cave and the girls reached the safety of the outer air.

They scarcely noticed that the rain had almost stopped and that the sky was brightening in the west.

They thought only of Hugh, in the cave with the venomous reptile that might, at any moment, thrash itself free.

Joe and Lloyd picked up several large stones just within the mouth of the cave, but Rose suddenly espied a rock that was bigger than any of them.

She hurriedly followed the boys back into the cave while Helen and Margy, each armed with a weapon, brought up the rear.

What followed was swift and certain and testified to the nerve and sure aim of Joe Morris and Lloyd Roberts. In a moment the head of the reptile was smashed beyond recognition while its body thrashed frantically about the place in the grip of muscular reaction.

Helen put a hand before her eyes and shuddered.

"I can't look at it any more!" she cried faintly. "I,—I think I need a little air—"

Hugh Draper left the forked stick stuck upright in the ground, put a hand beneath Helen's arm and led her gently from the cave. The others followed, sickened and a little unstrung in the grip of the reaction. It was then that they noticed the storm had spent itself.

"Oh, look at the sun! We'll have to call that a good omen," said Rose shakily.

"Maybe our troubles are over at last," observed Margy. "Perhaps now we can begin to enjoy ourselves."

They walked for a little way silently through the woods, looking for an open spot where the rays of the sun might have a chance to dry their wet clothing and where they might test the contents of the lunch basket which Joe had had presence of mind enough to rescue from the cave.

"Thanks be to the gods of the weather that it is so hot. It makes wet clothes rather comfortable than otherwise," said Margy.

"Good stars! who cares about wet clothes, anyway, after what happened in that horrible cave!" cried Helen. "I think you were splendid, Hugh," she added impulsively.

"So say we all of us," cried Rose, in high spirits once more, now that the danger was over.

"I'd really like to know how you did it, old man," said Joe, turning soberly to Hugh. "You trussed up that snake in the neatest kind of shape—and in the dark, at that."

Hugh shook his head.

"I caught him just before the light went out," he explained. "It was lucky, for in another moment I would have missed him—"

"And there would have followed one pretty
mix up," said Rose.

"But tell me," Joe persisted. "Where did
you learn that trick with the forked stick?"

Hugh smiled reminiscently.

"A long, long time ago," he said, "I used to
spend the summers in the mountains with an
uncle of mine. There was an old man up there,
an eccentric old fellow and a neighbor of ours,
who used to catch snakes—"

"What ever for? Was he crazy?" asked
Rose, wide-eyed.

The young lawyer shook his head.

"Far from it," he replied. "The old man
knew what he was about, all right. You see, he
used to sell the snake skins."

"Did he catch his prey with a stick like
yours?" asked Margy, keenly interested.

Hugh Draper nodded. "It was because that
forked stick looked so much like the one the
old snake hunter used to carry with him that I
had a notion to pick it up."

"Well, all I have to say," remarked Rose,
with a gusty sigh, "is that that was a mighty
lucky notion for us all!"

CHAPTER XIII

The Doorbell Rings

THEY had a great time after that, for Fate, having sent them so many mishaps, relented and made up for harshness by permitting them to find the very spot they wanted for their picnic and by sending a spell of good weather and some extra hot sunshine to dry them out in a hurry.

"I wonder what kind of snake that was," said Margy, meditatively munching a piece of sugar bun.

"We can go back and see, if you like," said Lloyd Roberts, grinning, and half rose as though to act on the suggestion.

Margy pulled him back with such energy that he very nearly fell in the lunch basket.

"For goodness' sake, be careful, Margy," protested Rose. "Don't ruin the lunch."

"To say nothing of me," added Lloyd, with a grin, as he reseated himself and reached for another sandwich.

They were so comfortable in their little grove that they might have stayed there until the shadows drove them out if Hugh Draper had not reluctantly reminded them of the swift passage of time and of the fact that boats leave on schedule.

They repacked what was left of the lunch and unwillingly abandoned the romantic glade and turned toward the boat landing.

"I don't want to go home!" protested Rose. "I'd like to camp out here and never see the inside of the Lossar-Martin store for the rest of my life!"

"Whenever you feel like that," Joe told her, "just think of the snakes!"

"Oh, aren't you horrid! I don't think you could have a romantic thought if you tried, Mr. Strainer Man!"

"Just the same, Joe is right about the snakes. I honestly prefer our uptown apartment—"

"Even with the musical Jamesons overhead?" asked Rose incredulously.

"Even with the musical Jamesons overhead!" returned Helen firmly. "Almost anything is preferable to snakes."

Rose giggled.

"Wouldn't the Jamesons like that?" she said.

"As much as I like the name of 'Strainer Man.' Where'd you get that name for me, Rose?"

Again Rose giggled.

"Have you forgotten the day we first met

and how, after you'd moved us all in, you came
dangling a poor, little kitchen strainer as a
last treasure?''

They reached the boat in good time and had
a delightful sail home in the cool of the evening. They sat in the bow of the boat, talking in
whispers, as though the beauty of the night
forbade them to speak aloud. The cool wind
fanned their faces; the mountains, etching an
irregular outline against the lighter background of a darkening sky, seemed suddenly
remote, infinitely mysterious.

Helen, sitting close to Hugh near the rail,
caught her breath in a queer little sigh. The
young man leaned forward, regarding her intently. Helen was a little like the mountains
to him, remote, always mysterious in her
dreamy abstraction. Hugh Draper felt that
she lived in a world of her own from which
ordinary mortals were denied admittance.
Perhaps it was because she was so different
from all the girls he had known that the young
lawyer found himself so deeply interested in
Helen Blythe, her hopes and aspirations.

Now he asked softly, as though not to disturb the current of her thoughts:

''One sighs for two things, happiness or sad-
ness. I hope you are not sad?''

''Oh, no,'' replied Helen quickly. ''I am
very, very happy. Who could help but be on
such a night as this? If I sighed it was because

I feel that I can never put upon canvas the thoughts I have, the pictures that are forever painting themselves for my eyes alone to see. Oh, if I could only show them to others as they seem to me—'' her voice broke and Hugh Draper put his hand gently over hers.

"I believe you will do that some day," he told her earnestly. "I believe that some day you will give to the world something it has never had before, something that is only yours to give."

Helen turned to him, her eyes shining in the darkness.

"Oh, do you think that—do you think that truly?" she asked eagerly, breathlessly.

Hugh's voice was husky as he answered gently:

"I do—with all my heart."

There was silence between them for a long time after that and then Helen said softly, as though speaking to herself:

"You don't know what it means to have some one's faith, some one's belief. If I do not succeed, at least it will not be because I have not tried."

A glamorous sail, a trip through all the romance and mystery of the world, and then, at the end, the lights of New York and—reality.

Nevertheless, the spell of the adventure was still upon them when they reached the little uptown flat, and when the boys said good-night

it was only after the girls had promised to let
them repeat the outing in a very short time.

The musical Jamesons were hard at work in
the flat above, but, despite their frightful
clamor, the girls fell asleep accompanied by
visions of cool, sweet-smelling forest glades
and moonlit waters flowing gently and eter-
nally between the mystery and majesty of
towering mountains upflung against a misty
sky.

Rose woke to the insistent ringing of an
alarm clock. It was Monday morning. Time
to get up and go to work. She flounced over
petulantly in bed; then impatiently stretched
out a hand and throttled the alarm.

"Oh bother!" she said, sleepily and aloud.
"What is the use of waking up anyway? And
it's going to be another blazing day. I wish I
could sleep forever!"

Realizing the futility of this wish, she flung
back the bed clothes and jumped resolutely out
of bed. Rose had long since found that the only
way she could get herself up at all, especially
on hot mornings, was to do it quickly, before
her resolution had time to weaken.

So now she slipped a kimono about her and
ran into the bathroom for her customary cool
plunge before dressing for the hard day's
work.

She could hear Margy moving about in the
next room and humming something beneath

her breath in her lovely, husky voice. Rose had always contended that her sister would have had an unusually beautiful voice if she had cared at all to use it. But Margy, the severely practical, scouted the notion, and could never, under any circumstances, be induced to sing for anybody.

Nevertheless, when in cheerful spirits, Margy sang as naturally and joyously as a thrush at sight of the sun, and the sound of the rich, golden notes never failed to thrill her younger sister.

"If I had a voice like that," she thought now, as she splashed and sputtered in the cold tub, "I would have it cultivated if it cost every last dollar I had in the world. Um-yum!" rubbing vigorously with a rough towel, "a cold bath does make you feel full of pep. I believe I could tackle any one this morning—even Mr. Henry Goos!"

Still feeling in splendid physical shape and reviewing happily the events of Saturday and their delightful restful Sunday, Rose dressed in a great hurry. It was not until she was combing out her lovely hair that she missed the ordinary morning aroma of frying bacon and coffee.

"Good gracious, I wonder if anything is wrong with Nell," she thought, brushing more vigorously at the gleaming golden curls. "She practically never oversleeps, like lazy me."

Rose knocked on the door of the larger of the two bedrooms which the two older sisters shared together and was informed by Margy that Helen had gotten up "ages ago."

With real misgivings Rose hurried to the dining room, realizing that there had been no sound of movement from that part of the apartment.

She stopped in the doorway and, finding herself unobserved, stared in amazement at her sister.

Helen was seated near the window, her sketching materials before her. She was completely absorbed in her work, oblivious, apparently, of anything that went on about her.

Rose came into the room softly, advanced on tiptoe and looked over her sister's shoulder. For a long moment she watched, marveling, while Helen sketched swiftly and surely.

Rose loved to see her sister at work. It always seemed like magic to her, the pictures taking form and shape and symmetry beneath the gifted fingers of the artist.

"Why, I believe it's a scene on the Hudson —something we passed Saturday!" She spoke the thought aloud and Helen started, half rising from her chair.

"Oh, it must be late!" she gasped. "And you haven't any breakfast. You poor child—"

Gently Rose pushed her back into the chair.

"You keep on with your work," she said.

"If you stopped now that wonderful thing might never be finished. You know that yourself."

Helen hesitated.

"But your breakfast—"

"I'll get that myself."

"You can't!"

"Just watch and see! You needn't think you are the only cook in the family!"

Margy came in at the moment and together the two sisters got breakfast, moving softly about so as not to disturb Helen at her work.

They were a little awed, for they had never seen their talented sister quite so absorbed in her work. Even when they were hatted and cloaked and ready to leave the house, she was still so oblivious of them that they would not disturb her, even to say good-bye.

"I hope she wakes up long enough to get something to eat," said Rose anxiously, as she and Margy parted at the subway station. "Will you be home to-night, Margy?" she asked as her sister turned away.

Margy hesitated.

"I don't think so," she said finally. "This is a very busy week for Miss Pepper, and that means that her social secretary will be very busy too. I think I had better stay at the Riverside Drive house for the next two or three nights, anyway."

"But suppose your inheritance comes from

Pogartown?'' Rose objected. ''The haircloth
furniture and flour box are due to drop down
on us almost any day now, you know.''

''In that case, I will beg a day off from Miss
Pepper and come and view my fortune,'' said
Margy gayly. ''Good-bye, Posie. I'll see you
as soon as I can, anyway.''

About three hours later Helen was roused
from her work by a sharp ring at the bell.
Running to the window she saw an expressman
before the door.

''The furniture from Pogartown!'' she said
aloud, her heart beating faster. ''Oh, I wish
Margy were here!''

CHAPTER XIV

HAIRCLOTH FURNITURE

THE two expressmen, a burly negro who looked like an ex-prize fighter and a white man, nearly as big, gruntingly and complainingly brought the furniture up to the small living room of the Blythe apartment and dumped it in the middle of the floor.

As nearly as she could tell—for the furniture was all crated and only by the size and shape of the crates was it possible to judge of their contents—Margy's inheritance consisted of a sofa, three large chairs, the big clock in a crate that looked uncomfortably like a coffin and the famous and mysterious box of flour.

When she had tipped the expressmen as generously as her very restricted means permitted, Helen looked around in dismay at the cluttered room.

"Hardly space to move about," she said aloud. "We were crowded enough before, goodness knows. And who, do you suppose, will open these crates?"

As there was no one present who could answer that question, Helen sighed and went back to her work. Margy's queer inheritance was very interesting, but at the moment, to Helen at least, it was not nearly so interesting as her picture—her "Isle o' Dreams."

Helen knew, as she sketched in the background of mountains, the rich foliage, the silver stream appearing broadly in the foreground, disappearing, reappearing again in the distance, a narrow ribbon, reflecting the brilliance of the sun, that this picture was the best she had ever done.

In a way, this effort differed from all her previous work. Heretofore she had always worked in the open, carrying her brushes and palette with her to some beautiful scene and painting what she saw. Now she was sketching from memory, reproducing one of those pictures forever painting themselves for her alone to see.

She could not visualize all the details of that beautiful view on the Hudson that had been her inspiration, but the picture itself was as clear to her as it had been at the moment she had seen it.

Working steadily, joyfully, she thought of Hugh Draper, of his generous encouragement and praise, and worked more eagerly still.

Perhaps he would stop in that evening. Perhaps he would look at her Isle o' Dreams and pronounce it good. She knew that it was good without his saying, but, with a curious eagerness, she wanted his praise.

When Rose opened the door with her latch key many hours later and nearly stumbled over the furniture in the front room, Helen realized that she had all but forgotten the arrival of Margy's queer inheritance. But at Rose's excitement and eager questioning, her own curiosity revived.

"When did it come?" queried the younger girl, as she flung off her hat and ran her fingers through the damp curls on her forehead.

When Helen explained that it had arrived before noon, Rose stared at her in astonishment.

"You mean to say you have had this stuff here nearly all day and haven't even tried to open a crate?" she asked incredulously.

"I haven't had time," Helen explained. "And, anyway, I couldn't possibly open those crates myself. It will take a man's strength for that."

"Give me a hard one!" Rose retorted, and was starting for the door when Helen caught her by the dress.

"Now where are you going, Whirlwind?" she demanded.

"To get a man, of course! What else?" And Rose jerked herself free and was out of the room before Helen could even open her mouth to protest.

The younger girl returned in a few minutes with Hugh Draper.

The latter looked interested. It was plain to see that Rose had told him the whole story in the few moments it had taken them to ascend the stairs together. He demanded to be shown "the inheritance" immediately.

They escorted him into the living room and displayed the confusion there. He stood looking down upon the crates meditatively, fingering his chin thoughtfully.

"To get those things apart will require the whole evening. I tell you what we'll do," he said. "Let's postpone this till after dinner and then we can make a regular party of it. What do you say?"

"Fine!" cried Rose, giving Helen no opportunity either to agree or protest. "And in the meantime I will telephone Margy and see if she can't come over, for the evening anyway, even if she can't manage dinner."

"That seems reasonable," replied Hugh. "Margy really ought to be here, seeing that this is her inheritance."

While Rose ran out to a telephone booth to call up her sister, the young lawyer turned to Helen and asked with interest if she had started her new picture yet.

"I have been working on it all day," she told him, and could not keep a tiny thrill of triumph from her voice.

"Are you going to let me see it, later?" he begged, and Helen nodded.

In a little while Rose returned with the announcement that Margy would be over after dinner, if nothing happened to detain her—like an "earthquake or a tornado or a wreck on the subway, or any little thing like that."

Rose was in wonderfully high spirits. After Hugh Draper had left to eat hurriedly his own dinner, she stood for a moment in wonder and admiration before Helen's new picture, then the younger girl insisted that she would get dinner.

"This is your day off," she told Helen firmly, when the latter protested. "Any one who can paint a picture like that has no business in the kitchen. You may set the table, though, if you like," she added, as a small concession.

"Thanks!" retorted Helen, and merrily set to her task.

Dinner was scarcely over and the dishes washed when the door was flung open and Margy dashed in upon them.

"Where's my inheritance?" she demanded. "Where are you keeping it? I warn you, you had better divulge the hiding place—"

Rose giggled.

"If we wanted to hide it we would have to hire another apartment," she said. "You talk as if it was a handbag or something."

"But where is it?" Margy insisted, and for

answer Helen took her by the shoulder and marched her, with the able assistance of Rose, back to the living room.

"There—gaze and be elevated!" commanded Rose, and then went off into another spasm of giggles at the amazed look on Margy's face.

"Good stars! I had no idea there was so much of it," cried the latter. "What in the world are we going to do with it?"

"That is the question that has been dismaying us all," Rose assured her. "But, seeing it belongs to you, the problem is yours, after all," she added cruelly.

Margy opened her mouth to retort, but a sharp knock at the door caused her to change her mind.

Hugh Draper was there and he had brought his mother with him.

"Oh, Mrs. Draper, how kind of you to come!" cried Margy.

Helen heard Margy's words and hurried into the hall, followed quickly by Rose.

"You're a peach, Mrs. Draper!" exclaimed Rose. Then, feeling that she should not have used such slang to the dignified lady, blushed, and stammered a quieter greeting.

Helen, too, greeted their guest cordially.

The girls were really delighted, for Mrs. Draper seldom went anywhere and it was a great compliment to them that she should consent to pay them this impromptu visit. She was a slight, sweet-faced woman who, since the death of her husband, had never lifted up her head. She had tried to resign herself to the inevitable for her son's sake, but the task was too heavy for her. Although she was always pleasant and sympathetic and interested in the troubles and joys of those about her, she seldom left her home except to go to market. She never invited any one to visit her.

Because of her son's intimacy with the Blythe girls and his interest in their struggles Mrs. Draper had come to know the three sisters very well, although this was the first time she had ever entered their apartment.

"I had to see Margy's strange inheritance," she explained, in response to Helen's cordial greeting. "My son seems to think that a real mystery surrounds it, and he has succeeded in arousing my curiosity."

"Mine doesn't need any 'rousing,'" Margy assured her whimsically. "I really believe I can't wait much longer to know the worst. Hugh, won't you please get busy with the hammer?"

Hugh smiled his quiet smile and reached for the tools.

"Anything to please a lady," he said. "Here goes!"

They watched eagerly, the girls occasionally lending their assistance while Hugh forced off the top of the biggest crate and pulled off some of the burlap wrapping.

"Margy first!" decreed Hugh, as the girls pressed eagerly forward. "She gets the first look."

"Well!" said Margy, after a long and comprehensive scrutiny of the crate's contents, "if you think it's any treat, come and see for yourself!"

CHAPTER XV

ANOTHER ASSIGNMENT

As a matter of fact, the first article of furniture, which was the large, old-fashioned sofa of the haircloth set, was anything but a thing of beauty.

When it was exposed to the full light of day —the rest of the crate having been knocked to pieces and transported to the kitchen—the girls were forced to admit that it was the ugliest thing they had ever seen.

"It may be comfortable, though," said Rose hopefully, and lay down upon it. She retained the recumbent position only a moment, however, and rose with a cry of distress as a protruding tuft of horsehair scratched her arm.

"The old thing's molting," she said crossly, examining the scratch. "I must say, Margy, I think your inheritance is a big joke."

"I myself begin to think poor Aunt Margy had a sense of humor," Margy admitted, but Hugh scouted their pessimism.

"Just wait a little while," he counseled. "I have a strong conviction that this old lady knew what she was about."

"Well, all right," replied Margy, though with no great degree of hopefulness. "Let's get on to the next crate."

The young lawyer worked swiftly and with as much precision as if he had been accustomed to opening crates all his life. In a surprisingly short time the entire atrocious set of furniture was exposed to the inspection of the distressed girls and Hugh had gone to work on the grandfather's clock.

This proved to be a rather good piece of furniture, though fully as old-fashioned as the haircloth set. When stood upright, wound, and set to ticking in a dignified fashion, it seemed quite friendly and companionable.

"Now for the can of flour," crowed Rose, when they had examined the clock before, behind, and all around. "I certainly am curious to see that can of flour."

But when the wrappings were removed from the last article of Aunt Margy's bequest the girls were forced to confess that it looked just like any ordinary can of flour.

It was a big can, and, upon closer inspection, it was found to be full to the top.

"Poor Margy," said Rose, sitting weakly down upon her heels and staring at her sister. "I'm mighty glad mother did not name me after poor Aunt Margy. Just think of the loaves and loaves of bread and the pans and

pans of biscuits you will have to bake before
you will get to the bottom of this can.''

''I feel lots more sorry for you, since you
have to eat them,'' chuckled Margy, but Helen
protested.

''Aunt Margy didn't say that in her will,''
she pointed out. ''She stipulated that you were
to do the baking, but she didn't say we had to
do the eating.''

''Oh, what an insult!'' cried poor Margy, and
then joined in the laugh at her own expense.

''What happens after you have baked up all
the flour and the rest of the family have either
eaten the result—''

''Or died of it,'' interposed Rose a little
wickedly.

''Or died of it?'' repeated Mrs. Draper, with
a smile in Margy's direction. ''Do you understand that when all this flour is used up the
mystery concerning this queer inheritance will
be solved?''

''That's just what we don't know,'' returned
Margy. ''All the lawyer said was that when
the flour had been baked into bread or biscuits
that we would hear more concerning Aunt
Margy's bequest.''

''Maybe she thought that by that time we
would all be dead of indigestion anyway, and
the money could go to charity,'' suggested Rose,
and Margy made a dive for her, tripped over
the grandfather's clock, and would have gone

headlong had it not been for Hugh Draper's long arm and his timely use of it.

"Now you see what you get," said Rose virtuously, from behind the protection of the couch. "Next time you try an act of violence, you had better watch your step!"

They spent some time discussing the disposal of the furniture. Obviously it could not all stay in the tiny living room, for there was not space enough between the pieces to permit of moving about.

Finally it was Mrs. Draper who solved the problem by making a kindly suggestion.

"I have room in my living room for the couch," she said. "And I could put one of the big chairs in the larger of the two bedrooms. That is, if you are sure you can't use them here."

The girls fairly fell upon her neck in gratitude. The remaining two chairs, the grandfather's clock and the flour box they could accommodate without serious inconvenience.

When the Drapers, mother and son, finally took their leave it was with the latter's promise that the couch and chair would be removed to the Draper apartment on the following day.

Not until Hugh had gone did Helen realize that in the excitement she had neglected to show him her new picture. She wondered at the keenness of her disappointment.

However, on the following day Hugh made up

for the omission by praising the picture with such genuine enthusiasm that Helen was completely satisfied. She felt that with his encouragement there was scarcely anything she could not do.

Finally came the night of Margy's first baking, and with it a great deal of fun and excitement. The great occasion fell on a date three days after the arrival of the "inheritance." It was the first chance Margy had had to get away from Miss Pepper and her rather arduous duties, and she was in hilarious spirits.

Margy was even less experienced in the art of cooking than Rose for, at their mother's death, the duties of housekeeper had naturally fallen upon the shoulders of the oldest girl.

But Margy was determined to follow the ruling of her Aunt Margy Blythe's will to the letter and so set to work dauntlessly to master this new and untried field.

The opening of the flour box was quite an event. Rose still harbored the belief that their eccentric aunt had hidden a wealth of Aladdin-like jewels in the flour and that they could expect to break a tooth upon diamonds and rubies with reasonable frequency.

She declared that she was really disappointed when the first careful sifting of the flour revealed not so much as a moonstone!

"Well, there's another hope gone," she grumbled, as Margy continued studiously to consult the cook book. "I'm through worrying about this crazy inheritance."

"Nobody asked you to worry," retorted Margy abstractedly. "All you need do is wait. Now, let's see—how much baking powder do you need?"

"Here it is, dear—can all open and everything," said Helen reassuringly, as she pushed an opened can of baking powder and a teaspoon toward the experimenter. "Just follow the directions in the book and you can't go far wrong."

"You don't know me!" warned Margy and evoked a burst of laughter from her unsympathetic audience.

In spite of the gloomy prophecies, the biscuits were not at all bad. Margy was not ambitious enough to try bread on this first occasion, but declared she would leave that "terrible deed" until some Sunday morning when she would have more time to learn how to "perpetrate it."

However, the first attempt was successful enough to cause Helen and Rose to predict that, with a little more practice, Margy would make an excellent cook.

"Practice is the least of my worries," remarked Margy, gazing ruefully at the flour box. "I am sure to get plenty of it. Just look, I haven't even put a dent in that flour yet!"

"It takes time, my dear, it takes time," said

Rose, adding soothingly: "Cheer up, honey, just think what mysterious and wonderful news awaits you when you come to the end of that flour box."

"Probably I will come to the end of me first," said Margy pessimistically, and was cheered and comforted by another hot biscuit which Rose passed to her.

"Think how much pleasure you'll be giving others, Margy," suggested Helen. "When you are at Miss Pepper's you can picture Rose and me feasting on the delicious bread you have worked so hard to bake."

Margy groaned, at which Rose giggled and said:

"Margy doesn't seem to take to the idea of doing a good in which she does not share in the results."

Whether it was the fault of too much hot bread or the truly remarkable chime of the great grandfather's clock, Margy did not know. At any rate, long after her sisters were sound asleep that night she lay awake, tossing restlessly on her pillow and listening, every hour and half hour, to the raucous voice of the clock.

As the hours passed there grew upon her the strange belief that if the old timepiece could speak it would be able to tell her that about its former owner and her strange bequest that would astonish Margy Blythe exceedingly.

The weird notion grew gradually into something bordering on obsession. Margy even went so far as to get out of bed and approach the clock, ticking away solemnly in the darkness. But she had looked at it only a moment when its rhythmic tick-tock seemed to change to a sing-song of her own name. "Margy Blythe, Margy Blythe, Margy Blythe—"

Margy turned and scuttled back to bed, calling herself all kinds of names as she did so.

"You are a perfect idiot, Margy Blythe," she scolded. "This mystery has your nerves wound up as tight as the spring of that clock. Now stop it, this instant. Do you hear?"

In spite of this severity, Margy never passed the grandfather's clock from that time until the solving of the mystery without a feeling that the piece of dead wood and machinery was more than half human!

The baking of the flour into bread proceeded slowly, perforce. Margy's duties as social secretary and her work at night school took toll of her evenings and sometimes of her week ends as well.

Meanwhile, Helen continued her work on the new picture, "Isle o' Dreams," at the same time, coloring sketches for the art dealer, Mr. Bullard, who was using a good deal of her work.

Rose went each morning, as usual, to the Lossar-Martin store, although the work under the iron rule of Henry Goos was becoming increasingly arduous. Rose watched Birdie North droop and wilt beneath the strain and did her best to shield the delicate girl. If Birdie had been the shirking type, it would have been easier to befriend her. But the girl had been accustomed for so long to taking more than her share of the work that she could not break the habit now, even though she cared to.

Meanwhile, Margy had again discovered the fly in the ointment of her contentment. The "fly" was Rex Pepper, the rich and idle nephew of Margy's employer and the same young man, who, upon a previous occasion, had caused Margy the loss of her position.

Rex Pepper admired Margy Blythe and did not care who knew it—including Margy Blythe herself. He had persisted in annoying the girl with his attentions, though she had repeatedly shown him how unwelcome they were.

It was only a day or two after the arrival of her queer inheritance from Pogartown, Iowa, that Margy heard a sound in the doorway and glanced up to see Rex Pepper standing there.

She rose quickly, an annoyed frown etching itself on her forehead while she hastily gathered up papers and manuscript.

"This time I've got the drop on you!" chuckled the big young man, and Margy glanced up at him, her eyes smoldering.

"I don't understand you," she said coldly.

"Well, you see, I happen to be completely fill-ing the doorway," Rex Pepper explained, with his broad, schoolboy grin that would have been disarming, had not Margy known it so well. "The only other way of escape is by the window, and if you tried that, you might attract attention."

"I am very busy, Mr. Pepper," said Margy. "I really haven't time to talk to you, or anybody."

"Especially me," said the big young man ruefully. "I say, haven't you forgiven me yet for taking you on that auto ride? I might apologize again," he added hopefully.

"Pray don't trouble," said Margy coldly, and would have said more had not Miss Pepper's maid, Jane, at that moment announced Mr. Elton. The young man, it seemed, was waiting to speak to Miss Pepper.

"He says he is a reporter and that he has an appointment with Miss Pepper," the maid said disapprovingly, and it was evident that her disapproval was for the journalistic profession and not for the appointment.

"Show him in," directed Margy. "I will see what he wants."

Rex Pepper looked at her reproachfully.

"I thought you were too busy to see any one," he said.

"This is business," Margy retorted coldly, and turned back to the desk to restore the papers upon it.

"Mr. Elton," announced Jane primly, and as Margy looked up her face lighted with genuine pleasure.

"Dale Elton!" she cried. "Why, how stupid it was of me not to know who you were at once!"

"And ungrateful, too," said Dale Elton of the *Evening Star,* coming forward smilingly to take her hand. "Especially since you were good enough at one time to credit me with saving your life!"

CHAPTER XVI

THE STRANGE MAN

"I BELIEVE your appointment is with my aunt?"

Rex Pepper had stood aside to let the young reporter enter. Now he spoke and his voice was so cold and strange that Margy looked at him in surprise. She had been accustomed to think of Rex Pepper as an overgrown, rather spoiled boy. But at the moment he looked anything but boyish. He was lounging in an easy attitude against the door casing but his mouth was drawn in a straight, thin line.

"Yes, it is," said Dale Elton, really noticing the young fellow for the first time. "I expect to see her, if she will be so good."

"Then I will tell her you are here," said Pepper, pleasantly enough, to all appearances.

But the angry light sprang to Margy's eyes again and she stepped forward quickly.

"I will call Miss Pepper," she said. "I believe that is my duty."

Her glance met that of Rex Pepper and in that instant the two crossed swords. Which would have won it is impossible so say, though it is probable Margy would have had her way in the end.

But at that moment an irritable voice was heard in the hallway and the redoubtable Miss Pepper herself appeared.

"What's this, what's this?" she queried! "Then, her glance falling on her nephew, she added angrily: "Haven't I told you not to come in here? Don't you know that this place is for Margy Blythe and my business. Out with you! Scat!"

"Beloved aunt," the youth began, but the little old lady turned upon him furiously.

"Don't you 'beloved aunt' me!" she cried. "Get out of here before I call Oliver and have you put out. Shoo! Scat!" With this admonition she deliberately turned her back upon him.

Rex Pepper scowled sulkily for a moment; then turned and sauntered from the room.

Dale Elton, who had been watching the scene with undisguised amusement, approached the peppery little old lady.

"I presume I am speaking to Miss Dorcas Pepper," he said. "I am Dale Elton, reporter on the *Evening Star*," he added, producing a card and handing it to her. "If you recollect, I had an appointment with you to discuss the things you are doing for charity."

Miss Pepper glanced briefly at the card, it seemed to fill her with an intense irritation.

"I don't have to talk to you," she fairly snapped at him. "Secretary here. Knows more about it than I do. Talk to her. I'm busy —very busy—very!" With this she turned and disappeared between the drawn portières.

Dale Elton stared after her and Margy chuckled at his expression.

"You mustn't mind her—really," she said, in a low voice. "She sounds awfully funny, but at heart she is the best little soul alive."

"You would have to prove that to me," said the young reporter, with an incredulous shake of the head. "In my profession I must meet all sorts and kinds. But, as an expert on the subject, I venture to say, without hesitation or fear of contradiction, that she is just about the queerest ever."

"But she really is wonderful," Margy protested. "Since you have come to learn about her work in getting up bazaars and other entertainments for charity, I will be able to tell you some things that, I think, will cause you to change your opinion concerning that little old lady."

"I wait only to be convinced," Dale Elton assured her, seating himself on a chair near her desk and watching her with undisguised interest. "I venture to say that if any one is able to change my mind, her name is Miss Margy Blythe."

"Her name is Miss Dorcas Pepper," said

Margy, with a whimsical smile. "You forget that I am to tell you about her—not about myself."

For half an hour Margy gave him the data his paper wanted concerning the social and club doings of Miss Pepper.

Finally Dale Elton snapped his book shut and returned it to his pocket.

"Now tell me about yourself," he requested, with his genial smile.

That sort of a request is the easiest one in the world to comply with, since most of us are eager, whether we are aware of it or not, to talk about ourselves.

Encouraged by Dale Elton's flattering interest, Margy told him almost everything of interest that had happened to her sisters and herself from the time they had last met, including the supremely interesting event—the arrival of her "inheritance"—before she was really aware that she had told him anything at all.

His increasing interest and the professional sparkle in his eyes suddenly warned Margy that she had gone farther—much farther—than she had intended.

"What a corking story!" cried the young fellow, with enthusiasm. "Human interest to burn. Eccentric old aunt, charming namesake, mystery surrounding inheritance. I say, just wait till the chief gets his eyes on this thing."

"But you never intend to put this in your

paper!'' cried Margy, suddenly aghast. ''Of course you wouldn't think of such a thing!''

Dale Elton stared at her for a moment, then shook his head in a gesture of utter dejection.

''You did this once before, young woman!'' he accused her, with mock bitterness. ''You wouldn't let me tell the world that I had saved your life—regardless of the fact that I did nothing of the sort!—and now you are trying to put a Maxim silencer on the slickest story I've heard in a dog's age. It's a hard, hard life—and I wish I were dead!''

Margy laughed unfeelingly.

''You will wish it still more if you ever put that story in the paper,'' she threatened, adding wheedlingly: ''Come now, give me your word that you will not put that story in your paper.''

''Lady, you have only to speak to be obeyed,'' he assured her mournfully and so despondently that Margy had an impulse to pat him comfortingly upon his head as one would a small boy who has been denied a stick of peppermint candy.

She resisted the impulse, however, and even regained her presence of mind sufficiently to remember that it was growing late and that she had still some work to do.

With this necessity to fortify her, she finally succeeded in reminding Dale Elton that he was not making a social call.

He rose reluctantly, still mournful, and would not leave until he had extracted from her a promise that he might visit the Blythe apartment on the next night but one for the purpose of viewing with his own eyes the ancestral furniture, the grandfather's clock, and the mysterious flour box.

"Though that is as nothing to the joy of seeing this marvelous story in print," he assured her sadly. "Lady, you have done me a great, great wrong. I can only hope your conscience will not trouble you."

"It won't!" Margy assured him, and inexorably showed him to the door.

Dale Elton appeared promptly at eight on the evening that had been set for his inspection of Margy's inheritance.

Helen and Rose greeted the young man with real pleasure. They had liked him ever since the day of their extraordinary meeting in Bronx Park and had been sorry when his work called him out of the city.

Elton regarded the two ugly pieces of furniture and the old clock—which he called "exhibits A, B, and C"—with a great deal of interest, and expressed regret that the other articles of furniture had been transferred to Mrs. Draper's apartment.

He inspected the box of flour also, but was forced to declare at last that he could make nothing of it and that it continued to remain a deep, dark mystery to him. Rose's theory of Aladdin-like jewels, he refused to consider.

"I must say, I'm beginning to agree with you," admitted Rose. "Not a tooth has been broken yet."

"Maybe your Mr. Hugh Draper's right, and when Miss Margy's learned to bake sufficiently well, J. Jones, Attorney, will write to say that her aunt's house is hers and that she's to come to Pogartown, Iowa, to run a boarding house."

Margy groaned. Then, to humor him and incidentally to get rid of a little more of the flour, she consented to make some hot biscuits while Dale Elton waited.

Helen brought forth some cheese and strawberry jam from the pantry, and the result was a little feast. Margy was improving with practice and her biscuits were really delicious.

"Say, I can see where you have a steady visitor from now on," prophesied the young newspaper man, as he helped himself to his fifth or sixth biscuit—he had long since given up count. "And if you don't want me around you mustn't make this kind of bread! I might even go to Pogartown to board with you," he added, with a cheerful grin.

Dale Elton was as good as his word and in the days that followed formed the habit of "dropping around" at the Blythe apartment quite frequently. But—and Rose was the one to notice this—he never came when he was not sure Margy was to be there. It was quite evident that Margy was the attraction as far as Dale Elton was concerned. And Margy continued to remain quite oblivious of his frankly expressed admiration!

The days moved on, with the contents of the flour box gradually diminishing. Dale Elton was not the only one who had formed a taste for Margy's bread and biscuits; Hugh Draper came often and Joe Morris and Lloyd Roberts, to say nothing of their girl friends.

Then, one day, something happened to startle Helen. The latter was busy about her work one day when she heard a slight noise in the hall of the apartment and went out to see if one of the girls had returned unexpectedly.

She went silently, for she always wore rubber heels about her work, and so was just in time to see a strange figure slip from the private hall of her apartment into the outer hall and close the door behind him.

More angered than frightened at the moment, she ran forward quickly and flung open the door. The intruder was half way down the first flight of stairs, but he turned quickly at the noise of the opening door. Helen got a good look at his face.

It was a peculiar face, and, for some reason, made her thrill unpleasantly. Her impression was of a mop of wildly upstanding, sandy hair, a wide, loose-lipped mouth and eyes that

stared strangely beneath jutting, sandy eyebrows.

She closed the door quickly, locked it, and
stood with her back against it. I was foolish to
feel so frightened, she told herself. The man
had probably gotten into the wrong apartment,
and, realizing his mistake, had retired with
more haste than dignity.

She would say nothing about it to the girls,
she decided. But she would be very, very careful always to keep the door fastened. She had
been careless about that, often slipping the
catch when she went out to market so she would
not need to get out her key.

Then a day or two later, returning from market, Helen found the door of the apartment
wide open. She had closed it tightly when she
went out, she was certain of that.

Who had opened that door, and how?

CHAPTER XVII

STOLEN

FILLED with forboding, Helen approached the open door.

Who had visited the flat during her absence? No one had a key but her two sisters and herself. Perhaps Rose had come home unexpectedly.

As she crossed the threshold Helen opened her mouth to call her sister's name, but closed it again on a strangled exclamation of dismay.

The living room was in complete disorder. Chairs had been thrown about, the center table pushed aside, and one of Aunt Margy Blythe's armchairs had been toppled on its nose and its legs were turned upward in a ridiculous suggestion of helplessness.

But Helen saw nothing at all humorous in the situation. She was genuinely frightened. Some one, a sneak thief probably, had entered the apartment during her absence, might even now be hiding behind a door or in a closet of one of the other rooms!

Helen half turned away, thinking she would call Mrs. Draper and ask her to help in the search of the apartment. But as she passed through the hall, her eyes fell upon the grand-father's clock and rested there in angry aston-ishment.

The door of the clock was wide open and the ancient timepiece had evidently been ransacked. It had been pulled out of place and thrown back-ward and rested against the wall in a dejected attitude. The ticking had stopped. For all Helen knew, the clock had been ruined by the mysterious marauder. She had come to have a real affection for the old clock, and now its dilapidated state changed her fright to anger and she resolved to search the flat without the aid of Mrs. Draper.

"If the thief came for money or jewelry, he must have gone away disappointed," she told herself. "But he might have taken the silver." She thought of the silver, her mother's prop-erty and special delight, doubly precious on this account, and hastened her steps toward the dining room.

It was not a pleasant experience, for she did not know at what moment some one might step out from behind a door. Helen made up her mind that, in such an event, she would not scream, whatever else she did, and walked on resolutely.

Nothing happened, and when she reached the

dining room, Helen found it undisturbed. Everything was just as she had left it.

After assuring herself of the safety of the silverware, Helen proceeded to make a more thorough search of the apartment, going slowly back through the rooms, poking into the depths of dark closets, looking under beds. This took courage, but, when aroused, the dreamy-eyed Helen had a great deal of pluck. Once started on a course, she would follow it through to the end, no matter what the cost.

The apartment was empty—that one thing was certain.

In the living room Helen picked up one of the overturned chairs and sat down in it. Not until then did she realize the great strain she had been under. She found herself trembling.

"It couldn't have been the work of a sneak thief, or something would have been stolen," she reasoned. "Unless I frightened him away," she added, on second thought.

But no one had passed her on the stairs. The intruder must have left the apartment house before she entered it—unless, at the sound of her approach, he had run upstairs instead of down.

The thought was not a pleasant one. Remembering suddenly that she had not closed the front door, Helen got up at once and proceeded to remedy the error.

"The thief may be still in the house," she said aloud, and shuddered.

Then she tried to think the thing out from another angle.

Suppose the intruder had not been an ordinary thief. Certainly the overturned furniture in the living room and the undisturbed dining room would seem to point to the fact that robbery was not the motive.

Why had the table and the chairs been flung about so recklessly? Why had Aunt Margy Blythe's furniture seen the roughest handling? Why had the poor old clock been ransacked so mercilessly?

Why? Why? Why?

Helen got up restlessly and went over to the clock. She righted it and gently set it going again. The works had not been damaged, it seemed; for, once restored to an attitude befitting its dignity, the old timepiece ticked on as comfortably as ever.

When Rose came home that evening Helen could hardly wait for her to remove her hat before telling the startling events of the day.

"Why, Nell, what an awful thing to have happen to you here all alone!" cried her sister. And you mean to tell me you searched the place by yourself? Why, you're a regular heroine! Just wait till I tell Dale Elton—you might get your picture in the Sunday supplement."

"If you dare!" cried Helen.

For answer Rose put an arm about her sister and drew her down beside her on the couch.

"You old silly! you don't suppose I'd do it, do you? Now tell me everything that happened all over again—and say it slow!"

But though they examined the mysterious intrusion from every angle, the whole thing remained as much a mystery to them as ever.

"Well, come along and let's eat dinner," said Helen, at last. She got to her feet and pulled the reluctant Rose up after her.

"I've put everything in the oven and I suppose it will be dried to a crisp—" She paused and a queer light came into her eyes. Rose was quick to see it an cried out eagerly.

"Nell! what is it? What's the matter?"

Helen put a hand on the younger girl's arm and regarded her oddly.

"I wasn't going to tell you or Margy, Rose, because I thought it would worry you. In fact, I had nearly forgotten about it myself. But the other day—"

"Yes, yes!" cried Rose impatiently, as her sister hesitated.

"I saw a queer man just slipping from the hall of our apartment."

Rose caught hold of the older girl's arm and shook it eagerly.

"Oh, Nell, you should have told me! What did he look like?"

Helen was able to give her a pretty good description, for the face of the sandy-haired man she had seen on the stairs was quite clear to her.

"I thought he might have found himself in our apartment by mistake," she said. "Things like that do happen, you know."

But Rose shook her head vehemently.

"I don't believe there was any mistake about it," she said. "And I would be willing to wager Aunt Margy Blythe's Liberty Bond that it was your sandy-haired man who did all this damage to-day."

Rose was reluctant to leave her sister alone in the apartment after that and suggested all sorts of wild plans, such as staying away from the store for a week and herself personally guarding the apartment.

When Helen would not hear of such a thing, the younger girl hopefully suggested the police, but Helen only laughed at her.

"Why, Posie, you are making a regular detective story of this thing," she accused the younger girl. "Whoever came here the other day is probably satisfied that we haven't whatever it is he wants and won't come again, Now stop worrying, dear. I'm all right."

But Rose did not stop worrying, and even went so far as to visit Margy at Miss Pepper's after work hours to tell her sister the whole story and ask her advice.

"Helen would think me crazy if she could see me now," Rose confessed, as the sisters sat in the lovely rose and gold room that was used by Miss Pepper's secretary. "She wouldn't hear of telling you for fear of worrying you. You know Helen."

"Yes, I know her!" said Margy fondly. "But I really believe with Helen, Posie, dear, that there isn't anything to worry about. Of course the whole thing is mysterious, but in all probability nothing of the sort will ever happen again."

"Just the same, I wish you could come home," said Rose wistfully. "I get uneasy and restless at night—as though something peculiar were going to happen. I think it is the striking of the grandfather's clock. It wakes me up on an average of twice a night, regularly."

Margy gave the younger girl a queer look.

"I don't like that striker much myself," she confessed. "There are times when I could take great pleasure in throttling it. Never mind; Posie," she added, in her cheerful matter-of-fact tone, "I am going to have this week-end off and I think I can manage to spend most nights of the following week at home, if you really want me. I'll bake some more bread, and maybe we will get to the bottom of the flour box. Who knows?"

Rose gave her sister a grateful hug and

pulled on her hat before the full-length pier glass that graced one side of the room.

"You always make everything seem all right, Margy," she said. "Now where are my gloves? Oh, never mind, I forgot I didn't wear any. No, don't bother to come down, dear. I ought to know my way out by this time. See you Saturday—if Helen and I aren't both knifed in our beds before then!"

The last was said laughingly, but long after her sister had gone Margy Blythe stared thoughtfully out over Riverside Drive and the gracious river beyond. In reality she was seeing a little apartment ruthlessly disordered by a mysterious hand, furniture overturned, a clock door open—

"I'll be glad to get home," she told herself finally. "It seems to me that there is more in this than meets the eye!"

One o'clock Saturday afternoon found Margy waiting for Rose at the Lossar-Martin store. Rose was always so pleased when one of her sisters called for her at the store that Margy had chosen this occasion to give her a pleasant surprise.

When Rose came out, accompanied by Annabelle Black and Birdie North, Margy was shocked by the appearance of the latter girl. She was so white and frail that Margy's heart was filled with pity. It seemed as though a breath of wind might blow the girl away.

Rose greeted her sister joyfully and announced that Birdie and Annabelle had agreed to run up to the apartment to have a "bread making spree."

"I had hard work persuading Birdie to come," Rose confided gayly as the four girls walked down the street together. "It was only when I promised that she might take Mother North a fresh loaf of homemade bread that she consented."

"Maybe Mother North won't thank me when she eats the bread!" said Margy ruefully.

But Margy's bread and rolls and biscuits turned out better than ever, and the girls were elated to see that the supply of flour was really getting low.

"I must say, I wish you'd bake your last batch of bread before long and find out what's at the bottom of this affair," said Annabelle as she buttered her fourth roll and ate it with relish. "Some people do have all the luck!"

The girls were inclined to agree with her when, on Sunday, just after the girls had come in from attending church, Joe Morris drove up before the door of their apartment house in a good-looking touring car and tooted vociferously outside the door.

Rushing to the window, the girls were in time to see Joe himself step down from the driver's seat with a lordly air, followed by Lloyd Roberts.

"And here comes Hugh, to see what all the noise is about," said Rose, with a delighted giggle. "Now I wonder who has come into a million dollars."

"The bus isn't mine, but it might just as well be," Joe explained a moment later, as he and the two other young men entered the apartment and confronted the curious girls. "The car belongs to the firm, but they as much as told me they didn't care what I did with it outside business hours. Care to come for a ride, girls?"

Did they care to?

In half an hour after the invitation they had packed a quick lunch of baked beans—in the can—boiled eggs, some of Margy's rolls, baked the day before, jelly, fruit and cake.

"We have enough for an army, but I reckon there won't be anything left to bring home at that," said Margy, as she gave one last look and slammed the cover shut.

It took the girls only a few minutes to dress, and they were soon rolling luxuriously through the crowded city streets toward upper New York and the open country.

Rose was in the front seat beside Joe and the other four were squeezed into the tonneau. There was no room to spare, but they were all too happy to mind a little inconvenience.

They reached the state road finally and Joe

"opened up," letting the machine speed up the even, macadamed road.

The girls could have ridden that way all day, but it was not long before the boys declared themselves famished. Joe slowed up and began to look about for some pleasant nook in which to assuage their hunger.

They found an ideal spot not far from a little roadside booth where soft drinks were sold.

"We'll get you girls settled and then walk back and purchase some of the stuff that cheers," said Hugh.

They ran the car a short distance from the main highway along a little, dusty side road, winding off across the hills. There they descended and, armed with the lunch basket, a blanket to spread on the grass, and other paraphernalia, they climbed a narrow, rock-strewn path toward the most ideal spot that was ever found for the enjoyment of picnickers.

"But we can't see the car from here," objected Helen. "Don't you think you had better pull it up a little further, Joe?"

"That little bus is as safe as though it was in church," scoffed Joe. "Come on, fellows. Now for some soft drinks."

They returned shortly and found the lunch all ready for them.

"Um-yum!" cried Lloyd, grabbing for a buttered roll. "You sure do know how to make the kind of bread grandmother used to make,

Margy Blythe. I say, how is the little old inheritance coming along, anyway?''

Margy told him that the supply of flour was
diminishing steadily and that she hoped soon
to learn something further concerning the mystery. In the lazy conversation that followed
the girls let slip something concerning the in-
vasion of the apartment, the overturning of
chairs and furniture, and the search of the old
clock. Both Joe and Lloyd were immensely interested in the story and indignant at the intruder—Joe declaring that if he ever got his
hands on the rascal, the latter would wish he
had never seen the light of day.

But Hugh Draper was really worried. He
did not like the idea of Helen's being alone in
the apartment all day after what had happened.
For, although he would not have alarmed her
by telling her so for the world, the incident
seemed to him like the work of a fanatic—a
crazy man, perhaps.

''I wish you would be careful to keep your
door latched,'' he said to Helen, when they were
clearing up, preparatory to leaving the spot.
''I wish you would promise me to be careful
about that.''

''I don't have to promise,'' said Helen. Although she spoke gayly, there was an undercur-
rent of earnestness she could not disguise. ''I
wouldn't leave my front door open for a hundred dollars!''

They started back slowly, sorry to leave the pretty place, yet eager to continue their drive.

Joe was the first to discover it.

"Look!" he cried, in a voice hoarse with consternation. "The car is gone!"

They stared incredulously for a moment, then began running toward the spot where the automobile had been just a short time before.

"Some one has stolen it!" cried Helen. "I knew we should stay where we could watch it."

"If some one has stolen it, then the thief must be near by," cried Joe excitedly. "Do you remember when I walked down the hill a few minutes ago? Well, the car was here then. Good-bye! I'm after the thief!"

He started toward the main road, but Rose called to him excitedly.

"Not that way, Joe! Come here and look at this!"

CHAPTER XVIII

ISLE O' DREAMS

ROSE was leaning down to examine something in the road and the others crowded around her to see what it was she had discovered.

"Sure enough, there's a fresh imprint of a tire," said Lloyd Roberts. "Your thief drove the car across country, Joe, instead of keeping to the state road. Come on."

They ran ahead, following the trail in true scout style. The dust was thick on the road and the trail was easy to follow because of a peculiar marking on the tires.

After a hot and breathless tramp they came finally to a group of farmhouses. Joe was approaching the first of these to make inquiries when he stopped, shouted wildly, then broke into a run.

Mystified, the others followed. Suddenly they saw what it was he pursued. A man dodged around one of the outbuildings, turned to avoid Joe, who was charging down upon him, and almost ran into the others, whom he had not yet seen.

144

Cornered, he turned again to double on his tracks when Joe shouted wildly to Roberts and the young lawyer:

"Catch that fellow! Don't let him get away! Grab him!"

Hugh and Lloyd both leaped forward, but Hugh was the first to reach the fellow. He caught him by the coat collar and held him, squirming, until Joe came up.

The prisoner was a dark-complexioned man, small and slightly built, but wiry.

Hugh had all he could well do at first to hold him, but as Joe approached the fellow turned suddenly sullen and quiet. He stood with his eyes on the ground, one heel digging into the dust of the road.

"I thought I couldn't be mistaken," said Joe, with a grim satisfaction that the girls did not understand at the moment. "Then car stealing business is your latest venture, is it? Come, own up, you sneaking cur. What did you do with my car?"

The fellow did not answer, but continued to dig his heel into the dirt. Joe wound a hand in his collar, jerked him away from his captor and, with one quick, powerful movement, forced him to his knees in the dirt.

"Now, will you tell me where you put my car? Or would you like me to hand you over to the first county constable we meet? I might as well tell you, Frenchy, that I know enough

about you to make even a country jail a pretty
uncomfortable place for you. Now then. Are
you going to be sensible or are you not?"

"You let me go and I tell you where ees the
car," the Frenchman muttered sullenly.

"You *show* me!" replied Joe grimly, and
jerked his captive to his feet.

The girls, who had been watching the scene
in intense mystification, breathed a sigh of
relief. They had been inclined to think that
Joe had allowed his imagination to run away
with him and they were very doubtful that this
queer fellow knew anything at all concerning
the whereabouts of the car.

They were, therefore, not only surprised but
greatly relieved when the captive started up the
road, Joe still holding grimly to his collar.

"I hope he isn't leading us into an ambush
or something," said Rose, who cherished a
great liking for detective tales. "Maybe we
will meet some of his friends further up the
road."

"Then I feel sorry for his friends," observed
Hugh Draper, a gleam in his eye.

"Me too!" agreed Lloyd.

However, the ambush failed to materialize.
Under the guidance of the surly Frenchman
they came at last to the machine, half overturned in a ditch by the side of the road.

"Lucky for us you don't know how to drive
a car, Frenchy," said Joe, giving his captive's

collar another twist. "You figured to be far,
far away by now, didn't you, and out of harm's
way—in my car, or, what is worse, in the firm's
car. I have a notion to give you one good lick-
ing before you leave us, you dirty little
scoundrel—just to remember me by!"

Before the girls could guess what he was
going to do, Joe drew back his fist and hit the
Frenchman a blow square on the point of the
jaw.

The man fell, but was up in an instant, as
agile as a cat.

Joe met him with another blow on the jaw,
harder than the first, that sent him sprawling
on his back in the dirt of the road.

The Frenchman lay there for a moment, as
though gathering strength, then scrambled to
his feet and set off in the opposite direction as
fast as his legs could take him.

Joe took a step forward as though to pursue
him, then turned back.

"Let him go, the little rat," he said disgustedly. "We've got the car, anyway."

"You seem to hate him a lot on such short
acquaintance," said Hugh Draper.

"Short acquaintance, nothing," snorted Joe.
"I've known that fellow for quite some while
and I don't mind saying right here that I never
knew any good of him."

Upon the persistent questioning of the girls,
Joe revealed the fact that the Frenchman had

run the little shop where Herbert Shomberg
had disposed of the feathers stolen from the
Lossar-Martin department store.

"But do you suppose this Frenchman knew
he was handling stolen goods?" asked Rose, her
eyes big.

"Know it? Of course he knew it!" snorted
Joe. "Why, that Frenchman was every bit as
crooked as Shomberg, only they couldn't prove
his guilt. If you have any doubt that he knew
those feathers were stolen, I should think this
day's work would remove it," he added. "The
minute I recognized that rat I connected him
with the stolen car—and you see how right I
was."

"I'll say you are right there with the detective work, Joe, old boy," said Lloyd admiringly. "You sure have missed your vocation."

The next problem was to get the car out of
the ditch. But as the road bed was hard and
the motor of the car unusually powerful, they
did not have as much difficulty as they had
anticipated.

In a few minutes the car was on the road
again. Joe turned it skillfully and demanded
that they all jump in.

They reached home about dark and had a
merry, pick-up supper in the Blythe apartment
and everybody pronounced it "the perfect end
of a perfect day."

This was the first of a series of drives in the

"firm's" car, and the girls soon came to know the scenery for fifty miles into New Jersey and New York State fairly well.

The hot weather had passed so quickly and, for the most part, pleasantly, that the first chill of fall days found the girls unprepared.

Even with their steady positions they had not saved very much from their salaries, and now they were faced by the problem of how to get warm clothing for fall and winter.

Rose and Helen decided to use the Liberty Bonds, Aunt Margy Blythe's legacy to them, for their own things, but poor Margy had not even that to fall back upon.

Miss Pepper was whirled into the feverish activity of fall, preparing in club and social circles for the work and fun of the winter, and Margy, as her social secretary, was busy all the time.

Rare were her visits to the little apartment now, rarer still those "baking parties" that had been so pleasant for them all. It began to seem as though Margy would never solve the mystery of her queer inheritance.

Meantime, Helen finished her picture, her loved "Isle o' Dreams."

She had finished also another assignment of sketches, given her to color by Mr. Bullard. The art dealer was a kindly old gentleman whom Helen had come to regard as her sincere friend.

Why not take her picture to Mr. Bullard and
get his criticism of it? He would tell her where
she had failed—if she had failed. And if the
picture was good, as she thought it was, he
would tell her that too, even more readily.

With a great deal of misgiving—and a good
deal of hope hidden away at the back of her
mind, as well—Helen carefully packed her picture, along with the finished prints, and went
downtown.

She found Mr. Bullard in his shop and cordially glad to see her. He praised the prints
too, telling her that her work was improving
steadily.

Then Helen began to take the wrappings
from her own picture and the white-haired old
gentleman looked at her curiously.

"What's this?" he demanded.

Helen flushed and would not meet his eyes
as she said, softly, breathlessly:

"Something of my own. Oh, I hope you will
like it!"

CHAPTER XIX

Ruined

Mr. Bullard studied the picture for a long, long time, while Helen went hot and cold by turns.

Then he took the picture and went to the door with it, where he could have a better light on its colors. Helen stood in the back of the store, hardly daring to breath, yearning for, yet dreading, his verdict.

Mr. Bullard turned to her finally, took off his glasses and wiped them carefully. She looked at him, eager, wistful, afraid.

"You have something there, my child," he said, with a little nod of his head to emphasize the words. "You have caught something very fine in that picture, something very elusive. It is not so much what we see when we look at it, as what we feel. The stillness, the breathlessness of earth and sky with your little island in the distance, holding its breath also, as though waiting for some great thing to happen; the only motion suggested, the rippling of the water as it winds its way through the mountains and the flight of birds in the distance. Yes, yes, you have depicted something there— a breathless hush, expectancy—My dear child,'' turning to her impulsively, hands outstretched, "I congratulate you!"

Helen felt the grip of those kindly hands and felt suddenly thrilled, exalted. As she stood there it seemed as though the gates of her ambition opened wide showing her a world that would some day acclaim her as this kindly old gentleman was acclaiming her now.

Through a sort of daze she knew that her companion was speaking and sought to concentrate on what he said.

"I shall want all of this kind of work you can do. I think I already have a market for this one—"

"Oh, then, you will take it?" Helen interrupted breathlessly.

"Certainly! Have I not just told you so?" asked the old gentleman, surprised. "And I will sell it for the best price I can get and take out only the usual commission."

Helen flushed.

"I didn't—understand," she stammered. "You have been so kind—all this has happened so suddenly—"

"You need not explain, my dear child. I know just how you feel." The old gentleman smiled down on her benignantly. "But, as I was saying, if you can bring me another origi-

nal picture within the next month, I think I
shall find a market for that, also.''

''Original pictures!'' murmured Helen.
''Oh, how I have longed for the time to come
when I might do my own work!'' The tears of
gratitude and joy filled her eyes and she
reached out blindly toward her friend.

''You are so very good to me,'' she said, and
stopped because she could not say another
word.

Mr. Bullard took her hand in his and patted
it gently.

''There, there,'' he said. ''You give me too
much credit. I am a very good business man,
that's all. Now, my dear, may I count on another picture soon? And I have some more
prints to be colored. Will you be able to do
those also?''

''I feel ready to promise anything now,'' she
said, smiling. ''I feel as though I could ac-
complish twice as much work as I have before.''

The old gentleman nodded sagely.

''Of course, Miss Blythe, you must not expect too much from a first effort,'' said the art
dealer. ''Only well known names command
good prices in the art world.''

''Oh, I'll be willing to take anything, so long
as you can sell it!'' she replied eagerly.

''I think I can get at least thirty dollars for
it—maybe more.''

''That will be fine!''

"Let us hope that some day your pictures will bring much more."

Helen did not notice the long journey uptown that day. She could think of nothing but her work and how soon she could start her new picture.

She had found out from Dale Elton how to go about obtaining a permit to sketch in the city parks. Having received her permit her thoughts turned now to Central Park, as being the one most convenient to her.

"If I can manage it at all, I'll go tomorrow," she promised herself. "If I start early I shall be able to get back before the crowd."

When Rose and Margy learned of their sister's good fortune they were wild with joy for her and immediately prophesied all sorts of wonderful and extravagant things concerning her future.

Helen went to the park the next day and, almost at once, found the subject she was looking for. She sketched that first day until the light changed, and every day thereafter for a week returned to the spot, working busily. By the end of that time the work was so far advanced that she could finish the picture at home.

Margy and Rose were all eagerness to see this new "masterpiece," as they insisted on calling it, but Helen stubbornly declined to let them see it, or even tell them the title of it, till it was completed.

"You will be able to judge it better then,"
she told them, and the girls were not able to
make her change her mind.

In the meantime Margy had managed to bake
one more batch of bread. Upon impulse, she
took a loaf of it to Miss Pepper thinking her
eccentric employer might like it.

Miss Pepper was evidently surprised at the
nature of the gift, but, as far as Margy could
see, she was not particularly overjoyed.

She turned the loaf over and over in her
hands, sniffed at it as though it were some particularly objectionable kind of cheese, and put
it down upon the table.

"Bad sign—begin to bake bread," she
pointed out to Margy, who was watching her
amusedly. "Points to matrimony. Better stop
it. Waste of time!" And went on dictating in
her usual disjointed manner.

But Margy noticed that she did not ring for
Jane and have the loaf of bread sent down to
the kitchen, but very carefully took it with her
when she went upstairs and carried it up to her
own room.

"She means to sample it secretly when she
is all alone, funny old soul," Margy prophesied, as she whipped her jumbled stenographic
notes into some sort of coherency. "I reckon
she will be coming back for more before long."

In this she was right, for the very next day

Miss Pepper broached the subject in her abrupt way.

"Good bread!" she said, and it took a moment for Margy to bring her mind back from the details of a charity ball in order to find out what she was talking about. "Very good, very good indeed. Splendid cook, my dear."

"Oh, I am glad if you liked it," said Margy, dimpling behind her pad. "I'll bring you some more to-morrow if you like."

"Oh, no—no!" cried Miss Pepper in alarm. "Too much fresh bread bad for digestion, very bad. Not to-morrow. Next day—day after. Not to-morrow!"

In spite of the qualification, Margy knew that Miss Pepper had thoroughly enjoyed the bread and was looking forward to having more of it.

"Well, she may—at least until Aunt Margy Blythe's flour gives out," said Margy. "I only wish it would give out!" she added impatiently.

Meanwhile, things were not going at all well for Rose and her friends at the Lossar-Martin department store.

Henry Goos was more of a martinet than ever. Already he had secured the discharge of several of the girls in his department for trivial offenses, and those who remained could not tell from day to day but what the ax might fall upon them next.

"He is just like an ogre," grumbled Rose,

after one of those occasions when Henry Goos
had reprimanded her for something that was
not her fault at all.

"Ugh! I'd like to throw something at him,"
said Annabelle Black, glaring at the thin back
of the floorwalker. "Sometime," she added,
with a sigh, "I am going to forget I'm a perfect lady, and do it!"

The girls giggled, all except Birdie North,
who seldom laughed these days. Birdie needed
all her energy just to keep on working.

Then, suddenly, things began to happen in
the Blythe household—many things!

Helen had been working busily on her picture
when she realized that her supply of paints was
getting low. Reluctantly she left the canvas
on the easel and started downtown to a store
she knew where she could get just the colors she
needed.

On the way home, she decided to do her marketing for the next day while she was out, and
then not have to come out again in the morning.

In the grocery she met the mother of the
"musical Jamesons" and chatted with her for
quite a time, while they chose vegetables and
eggs and discussed the different brands of
coffee.

It was all very pleasant and chummy and,
as Mrs. Jameson accompanied her, Helen did
not hurry on her way back to the apartment.

They climbed the stairs together and Mrs.

Jameson went up to the flat above while Helen cheerily fitted the key in the lock.

She was humming a little tune as she entered the apartment, but one glance at the interior froze the song on her lips.

Helen passed a hand before her eyes to clear her vision. Then her face whitened and her lips compressed in a thin line.

The mysterious vandal had been at it again —only more thoroughly this time.

The furniture stood in a huddled heap in the center of the room. Torn papers, books and magazines were strewn broadcast.

Helen went into the bedrooms and found the drawers of the dressers wide open, their contents tumbled out on the floor.

She did not stop to straighten up, but hurried into the dining room. She had thought suddenly of her picture, almost finished, standing on its easel.

At the door of the dining room she pressed a hand tight against her mouth to stifle a cry.

There on the floor lay her picture, slashed through and through with fiendish thoroughness, the canvas hanging in strips. A very sharp knife had been necessary for that piece of work, and unconsciously Helen glanced backward as though she dreaded to feel the cold steel of it between her shoulders.

She looked at what had been her picture and sank to her knees beside it, sobbing. She took it up gently and covered it over as though it were some poor mutilated thing she could not bear to look at.

A light quick step sounded in the hallway, and Helen whirled quickly about.

Rose was in the doorway, her eyes wide, two vivid spots of color burning in her face.

"Nell!" she cried, advancing with out-stretched hands. "What is it? What has happened?"

CHAPTER XX

The Trap

HELEN removed the cloth from the picture, pointed voicelessly to the pitiful remains of her work. Even then she could not trust herself to speak.

Rose came closer and put an arm about her older sister.

"You poor dear!" she said softly. "And after all your work! But who—" she flung away from Helen, her cheeks blazing feverishly, her eyes gleaming with anger, "who did this terrible thing? Why, the whole place is pulled to pieces! I could see that as I came through the hall."

Helen nodded and again carefully covered her picture.

"The same one who was here before I suppose," she said slowly. "Only this time he—he found my picture. I—oh, Rose—it seems as though I couldn't stand it!"

"There, there, don't cry, honey," soothed the younger girl, her own eyes brimming with tears. "We'll find that wretch if it takes a hundred years!"

"By that time I won't be able to paint any more pictures!" said Helen. And then, because it sounded so ridiculous, she began to laugh, and felt a little better for it.

"Listen!" cried Rose, beginning to drag her sister through the hall toward the upset living room. "I have something to tell you that will make you open your eyes wide."

"For goodness' sake, what now?" cried Helen, for there was an excitement in the younger girl's voice that filled her with a new alarm. "If I have to hear any more bad news, I will give up!"

"Well, you may not think it bad news, but it certainly is interesting," said Rose. "Helen, the Drapers' flat has been ransacked too in much the same way as ours—furniture all about, drawers open and their contents scattered to the seven winds. Nothing stolen though—the silver is all there and Mrs. Draper found her jewel box on the floor with none of its contents touched. Now, what do you think about that?"

Helen stared at her sister incredulously.

"Why, Rose, I can hardly believe it! How did you find this out?" she asked quickly, started on a new train of thought.

"Met Hugh on the stairs as I was coming in," replied Rose. "He was on his way up here to see if you had been annoyed. Then his mother called him for something and he went

back. I expect he will be up any minute."
Just then their doorbell rang. "There he is
now!" and Rose ran and admitted the young
lawyer.

"Oh, I'm glad you came, Hugh!" Helen's
voice was frightened and appealing, like a little child's. "We need you so much!"

Hugh came in, cast a comprehensive glance
about him, and, coming over quickly, took one
of Helen's hands in his.

"Did you come in alone after this happened?" he demanded.

Helen nodded.

"I went downtown for some paints, then did
some marketing, and when I came back things
were as you see them," she said.

Still holding her hand, Hugh seated himself
on the couch beside her. He was frowning
thoughtfully.

"Mother was out too, and when she came
back she found the apartment in a pretty bad
state. Everything turned upside down, but not
a thing missing."

Rose had been watching him intently while
he spoke. Now she cried eagerly:

"You have something up your sleeve, Hugh
Draper—some plan!"

The young lawyer shook his head.

"Not a plan in the world," he assured her.
"Merely an idea. Has it struck you as at all
peculiar," he added, addressing himself di-

rectly to Helen, "that both times this fellow, whoever he is, has committed his depredations, he has seemed chiefly concerned with Margy's queer inheritance from her Aunt Margaret Blythe, of Pogartown?"

Both girls started and looked at him intently.

"You believe, then," said Helen slowly, "that if your mother had not taken some of that furniture into her apartment, she would not have been annoyed?"

"Events seem to point that way," replied Hugh. "Especially since the motive was not robbery."

They were silent for a moment, thinking this over.

"Supposing this is so, what plan have you in mind, Hugh?" asked Helen. "Do you think we ought to inform the police?"

Hugh hesitated then slowly shook his head.

"I don't think so, yet," he answered. "It seems evident that the fellow who has done this thing is a fanatic, and people who are a little off in their heads are usually easy to catch. I have a great longing to set a trap for this fellow myself."

"What would you do?" asked Rose breathlessly.

Helen said nothing, but her eyes were intently fixed upon Hugh's face. She seemed to realize for the first time that he held her hand, and gently withdrew it from his clasp.

"Just get Helen and my mother to go out some day—not together, as that would arouse suspicion in the mind of our desperado—and stay away for several hours. During that time, I will be hanging around to watch developments."

"But how do we know the fellow will be around at that particular time?" objected Rose.

"We don't," replied Hugh promptly. "We would have to take a chance on that. And if the trick didn't work the first time, we could try again, and yet again, if necessary. At any rate, I am going on the assumption that our friend, like most fanatics, has a one track mind and that that mind is at present centered upon Margy's inheritance from Pogartown. In that case he will probably hang about here pretty steadily. Meantime," Hugh got up an glanced about the cluttered room, "I am going to put this furniture back in place for you girls before I go down and do likewise for mother."

At the door, a few moments later, Hugh turned gravely to Helen.

"Are you keeping your promise to me?" he asked. "Do you keep your door locked during the day?"

"What difference does it make?" said Helen ruefully. "Our friend seems to have a duplicate key!"

Hugh scowled and his hands clenched hungrily.

"The scoundrel," he growled. "I'll get him, if I have to watch this house for the next six months!"

At the store the next day everything went wrong with Rose. Henry Goos seemed to hover constantly near her counter, and under his critical eyes she made mistakes that would have been impossible under ordinary circumstances.

"Say, you want to watch your step, Posie," said Annabelle, after hours that day, when they were putting the merchandise away for the night. "I have a theory about that bird, and I bet it's the right one, too."

"What do you mean?" asked Rose listlessly. She was chagrined and humiliated because of the frequent reprimands she had received that day, and was not anxious to hear any of Annabelle's theories, interesting though they frequently were.

"You know he tried to make up to you in the beginning," proceeded Annabelle, not in the least chilled by her friend's indifference. "You got to expect that, Posie, with your particular kind of looks—"

"I wish I was as homely as a stone fence!" cried Rose, at the end of her patience.

"Now you're just talkin'," returned Annabelle calmly. "Nobody wants to be homely that hasn't got something loose in the upper story.

Anyway, when you gave our friend Goosey
the glassy eye, he right away makes up his
mind to return the compliment with interest.
Get me?"

"Oh, I get you well enough," returned Rose
wearily. "You are only telling me what I
know, Annabelle—"

"Yes, but here's the joker in the pack," in-
terrupted Annabelle. "Who do you suppose
I saw last night with a swell girl on the White
Way but our little friend Goosey."

Rose's eyes widened.

"You mean," she hazarded, "that you think
Henry Goos has a girl friend he wants to get
in, in my place—"

"Right the first time, dearie," said Annabelle cheerfully. "I have to give you credit
for a lot of brains. Now let's be going, or that
bird will find us talking and fire us out of hand.
My, but I love him something fierce!"

Although Annabelle's theory concerning the
reason for the floorwalker's treatment of Rose
might seem a trifle far-fetched, Rose came to
believe more and more as the days went by that
it was a correct one. Henry Goos would not so
persistently single her out for reprimand and
criticism if he had not some definite object in
mind. The situation was all the more exasperating since, in her heart, Rose knew that she
was as efficient as any girl in the department
and a great deal more efficient than some of

them. However, as she herself said, there was little she could do, save "hold tight and hope for the best."

Meanwhile, Helen found that by carefully piecing together her ruined picture she could restore it to its original outlines sufficiently to permit of her copying it upon a new canvas.

This she undertook to do, working with a feverish energy in the hope of making up for the time she had lost.

During these days Hugh Draper was working hard at several law cases he had on hand. This work must be cleared up before he could set the trap for the fanatic who had so disturbed them all.

Then one evening he came to Helen and asked her if she could arrange to leave the apartment alone for the better part of the following afternoon.

"Mother has arranged to visit a friend of hers for the day," he explained. "And if you can go out also, it will give our friend a fine chance to stage another of his little raiding parties. Only this time, I will' be on hand to put a spoke in his wheel! I can bring home some work, and won't go downtown at all during the day."

Helen said that she would run up to see Margy at Miss Pepper's and perhaps stop in to see how Rose was getting on at the store, too.

Then, if she still found time on her hands, she would stop in and see a moving picture.

"Fine!" approved Hugh. "I will get the rascal this time, or know the reason why!"

The next day was an exciting one for the whole Blythe family.

Margy, at Miss Pepper's had been informed of the "trap" and of Helen's proposed visit to her. And Rose was so excited and nervous that she could scarcely keep her mind on her work, and for once gave Mr. Goos cause for his criticism.

As soon as she had finished the housework, Helen unable to wait for afternoon dressed quickly, put the new picture carefully away, and locked up the apartment.

She knocked gently at the Draper apartment and slipped the key under the door. Hugh, on guard on the other side of the door, picked up the key and put it carefully in his pocket.

Mrs. Draper had gone out early. In the course of the afternoon the young lawyer locked up ostentatiously and himself went out.

But Hugh did not go far!

Meanwhile, at Miss Pepper's, at that lady's insistence Margy and Helen had a delightful lunch together, which neither of them could properly enjoy because of their excitement.

"I don't see how I can possibly kill time until evening," sighed the older girl. "I'll run down to see Rose now, but I'd much rather go straight home.''

The visit to the store was a disappointment too, for the floorwalker hovered so close to Rose all the time Helen was there that the sisters scarcely had a chance for a word together.

At last, fearing that she would do her sister more harm than good by lingering, Helen said good-bye and hurried out.

She went straight from there to the nearest moving picture house, resolved that she would keep her promise to the letter and not return to the apartment until the time agreed upon.

As the hours slipped by she gradually felt herself oppressed by a premonition of evil. When the time was up and she felt herself at liberty to return home, she raged at the crowds that held up traffic in the subways.

Once arrived at her station, she ran all the way to the apartment house; arrived, breathless and frightened, to meet Mrs. Draper at the steps.

''Oh, have you been inside?'' gasped Helen, seizing the older woman's arm eagerly. ''Hugh is all right? Nothing has happened to him?''

''I haven't been in yet,'' replied Mrs. Draper, as they hurried up the steps together. ''I have just returned after a perfectly endless day. The hours were interminable.''

Helen nodded.

''It has been the same with me,'' she said.

"I never tried to kill time before, and I can't say that I like it."

"No sign of Hugh—everything seems quiet enough here," said Mrs. Draper, as she fitted the key in the lock of her apartment.

Helen stepped inside long enough to see that the first floor apartment was in order. Everything was exactly as Mrs. Draper had left it in the morning and the older woman breathed a sigh of relief.

But Helen was not satisfied. The premonition of disaster was still strong upon her. She bade Mrs. Draper good-bye, and, turning, hurried up the stairs toward her own apartment.

As she reached the bend in the stairs, her heart stood still and she clutched at the railing for support.

Some one was standing in the open doorway of her apartment—some one who swayed dizzily and seemed about to fall.

"Hugh!" she cried, recognizing him suddenly. "Oh, what have they done to you? What have they done?"

CHAPTER XXI

HUGH TELLS A STORY

"PLENTY!" said Hugh, with a wry smile, in reply to Helen's cry, as the girl ran to him and put an arm about him to steady him. "Better ask what they didn't do to me—or, rather, he! Just one man knocked me out cold, Helen. Can you realize that? I'll never get over it!"

"Don't talk about it now," urged Helen, leading him toward the living room. "Sit down and when you feel better you can tell me all about it."

As she pushed him into one of the big chairs, Helen found she was trembling in every limb. It was then she noticed that he was bleeding from a long cut on his forehead.

"Wait a minute!" she said. "I'll be right back," and darted from the room. In a moment she returned with a basin and bandages.

Hugh looked at her curiously. He was still a little dazed from the blow on his head.

"Why all the Red Cross preparation?" he inquired. "I'm all right."

"You will be, when I get through with you,"

Helen retorted briskly, as she dipped a wad of cotton in the water and began to bathe the wound gently. "I dare say, you don't even know you are bleeding," she scolded.

"I shouldn't be surprised at anything," returned Hugh. He closed his eyes and gave himself up to her gentle ministrations. "My, but you make a good nurse, Helen! I'd get banged up all over again for this!"

"Hush," chided the girl, as she put some healing powder on the cut and wound a bandage around his head, neatly holding it in place with some pieces of adhesive tape. "You needn't get so careless with your head."

"Why not? It's perfectly useless," grumbled Hugh, dimly conscious that his head was aching rather badly. "To-day's events prove that."

Helen took the bloody basin from the room, washed her hands, and returned to Hugh. Drawing up a chair close to him, she asked, eagerly:

"Just what did happen, Hugh? You can tell me all about it now."

"I can, but I don't want to," returned Hugh, closing his eyes again and frowning beneath the bandages. "The joke was all on me. You see, it was this way," as Helen made an impatient movement. "I was watching both apartments, and when hours went by and nothing happened I had about decided that the game was up—for to-day, at least.

"Then, late this afternoon, just a little while before you came home, in fact, I saw a sandy-complexioned individual slip into the hall and go up the stairs like a shot. He'd pressed the buzzer for one of the top-floor flats, I think, and got in that way.

"I waited a minute till he had disappeared around the bend in the stairs; then followed as cautiously as I could. When I came to your apartment the door was closed and the place was as still as death.

"I thought at first that the fellow might have gone on up to the next floor, but I decided that he would not have had time to do that, without my catching a glimpse of him.

"As quietly as possible, I opened the door with the key you had given me, and stood just within the door, holding my breath to listen. If I had heard the slightest sound to guide me, I might not have behaved as foolishly as I did."

He paused for a moment reflectively, and Helen edged closer to him.

"What then?" she asked softly.

"Then came the beginning of the end," Hugh told her, with the same wry grin. "I was moving cautiously across the living room toward the portière between it and the dining room, when it seemed to me that the curtain swayed outward with the barest perceptible motion."

"Oh," the girl cried and unconsciously

moved nearer to Hugh and away from the portière. "What did you do then?"

"You might better ask, what did *he* do?" Hugh retorted grimly. "I had gathered myself to spring upon that curtain when it was flung aside and I caught a glimpse of a sandy-haired demon catapulting through the air toward me. Then next moment I felt a vicious crack on the head and—as they say in stories—knew no more! You don't have to be told the rest of it, for I had just recovered consciousness and got as far as the door when you came up the stairs."

There was silence for a moment. Then Helen got up and pushed the curtain back as far as it would go.

"I know it's foolish," she said, in response to Hugh's look. "But I feel safer that way."

Hugh did not laugh. He continued to look grave and motioned her back to the chair.

"We have kept this from the police so far," he told her slowly. "But I guess the time has come when we shall have to ask their help. I certainly shall not have an easy moment until this rascal is caught and a stop put to these annoyances."

He got up unsteadily and Helen put out her hand quickly, solicitously.

"You ought to rest a little longer, Hugh. Please!"

"I'm all right," he told her gruffly. "I am

going to call the police and ask them to send a detective up here.''

So it came to pass that Margy and Rose, arriving home together, were treated to the sight of a plain-clothes man calmly going over their apartment.

Rose gave one look at Hugh's bandaged head and promptly went into a mock faint, from which she was rather rudely roused by Margy.

''Can't you see this isn't any time for joking?'' rebuked the latter, a bit sharply. ''Can't you see that something serious has happened?''

''Poor Hugh!'' returned Rose, with an irrepressible gleam in her eye. ''I bet he thinks it has!''

But when Rose learned the facts of the case she lost all impulse to laughter. Here, indeed, was something as menacing as it was intangible and mysterious; something that needed to be cleared up at once.

But though the detective from headquarters asked innumerable questions and looked very wise, he could throw no light on the mystery.

''We'll get busy and dig up some clues. And meantime we will have the place watched day and night. If the fellow should come back again, he'd find himself in a pretty trap. It's my opinion,'' he lowered his voice to an impressive whisper, ''that this whole business is the work of a nut, and nuts are easy to catch.''

Almost Hugh's words, exactly, and yet—the "nut" was still at large!

"He's after your inheritance, all right, Margy Blythe—the 'nut,' I mean, not the detective," said Rose when, the detective gone, they were trying to put the flat in order. "Next thing you know, he'll go off with Aunt Margaret Blythe's chairs on his back!"

"I wish he would take the flour box, too," grumbled Margy. "I am sick to death of making bread!"

Nevertheless, she baked another batch that very night, for she was filled with an intense eagerness to get to the bottom of that flour box. With her sisters, she shared the belief that, that task accomplished, they would very quickly learn the answer to the mystery which had been baffling them so long.

"I tell you what we can do," suggested Rose a while later, as she rather listlessly buttered a slice of bread—for even homemade foodstuffs can pall when one gets too much of them! "Why not give a 'biscuit party' and invite everybody we know to it? By the time you have fed them all, you ought to have reached the bottom of the box, Margy. How about it?"

"It's a great idea, if I live through it," agreed Margy. "Let's set the date for next Saturday night and get the agony over with."

"Poor Margy! You will have to spend all evening in the kitchen," said Helen. "Although I would be only too glad to help in the baking, if you would let me," she added tentatively.

"Me, too!" said Rose, with her usual disregard of grammar. "I'd do anything to find out what Aunt Margy was driving at when she made that silly old will."

Margy stubbornly shook her head.

"It was distinctly stated that *I* was to bake the bread," she said. "And I'll do it, if it kills me."

Once the party date was set, preparations for it went ahead rapidly. Everybody was invited by telephone or in person the very next day, and everybody accepted at once. For the Blythe girls were already famous for their parties and no one ever missed an affair given by the trio, if it was humanly possible to get there.

Also, the mystery of Margy's queer inheritance had roused the curiosity of the young folks and they looked forward eagerly to a possible solving of it.

"I know what I'd do," said Rose. "As soon as all of the flour is baked up I'd send a telegram to J. Jones, Attorney, and make him aware of that fact."

"Oh, I'll let him know, don't worry about that," answered Margy. "But I guess I'd better write him a letter."

Meantime, the weather grew so suddenly

cold that there was no longer any possibility of putting off the problem of warmer clothes.

Both Helen and Rose hated the thought of using their Liberty Bonds for the purpose. Rose had more reason for her reluctance than her older sister, for, with the instability of her position at the store and the antagonism of Mr. Goos, the girl felt that she needed the money as a buffer against the rainy days that seemed so imminent.

Still, it was more sensible to spend the hundred on warm clothes than to pay it out in doctors' bills, and a business girl must be properly clothed.

So, reluctantly, Helen and Rose parted with enough of their slender inheritance to buy a winter suit apiece, shoes, gloves, and hat to match. It was surprising how much things cost even when one shopped as economically as possible!

After a great deal of consideration, and examination of her tiny bank balance, Margy decided that her old suit would have to do. The suit was warm, and, against that obvious advantage, what did a few shiny places and a patch matter? And all the time, brave as she was, in her heart, Margy Blythe knew that the patch did matter, oh, very much indeed!

Margy got leave of absence for all day Saturday and spent it—as she grumblingly said—

working harder than she ever did at Miss Pepper's.

Part of the day she helped get the house in order for the party, but all the afternoon she spent in baking.

"I'll have to make the biscuits the last thing after they get here," she said. "But thank goodness I can get the bread and rolls off my hands ahead of time."

At last everything was in readiness and it was time to dress.

Helen finished first, and when Rose came out a few moments later she found her sister sitting in the dark living room, staring out of the window.

"Goodness, why don't you put on the lights?" cried Rose. "You look like a ghost, sitting there."

For answer Helen drew her sister toward the window; pointed to the figure of a man on the opposite side of the street. While they watched, he walked back and forth, back and forth, several times, like some sentry at the battle front, keeping watch; then stopped within the shelter of a doorway to light a match.

"Do you see that man?" asked Helen, in a low voice.

"Since I have not suddenly been stricken blind, I suppose I do," Rose answered flippantly. "What of it?"

"He is the detective from headquarters,"

said Helen, still in that low, tense voice. "He
has been here every night since Hugh called up
the police."

"Well, I should think you would be glad,"
said Rose, resenting the strange chill that crept
over her. "We are a great deal safer with
somebody watching the house. If Mr. Sandy
Hair comes back again and tries to act funny,
he is likely to find a surprise waiting for him."

"I know. But it keeps the whole thing before
me so," said Helen. "I never go out and come
into the apartment again but what I expect to
be met by some one. I never go past that portière without imagining that I—that it—"

"I am going to put on the light," cried Rose,
jumping up. "In about two minutes more you
will have me shivering too, Helen Blythe.
There!"

She pressed her finger upon the switch and
the room was suddenly flooded with light.

At the same moment, a peal of the front
doorbell announced that the first guests had arrived.

CHAPTER XXII

More Mystery

In the excitement and fun of welcoming their friends the girls were able for a time to forget the silent sentry, marching back and forth across the street.

The guests included Dale Elton, Betty Roberts, Lloyd's sister, Birdie North and half a dozen others of the girls' business acquaintances, besides their more intimate friends.

As Margy looked at the gathering, she was prey to a panicky fear that she had not made biscuits enough for such a crowd.

Her fears proved groundless, however, for even that group of hungry young folks could not dispose of the quantities of hot bread and honey Margy put before them.

Dale Elton was at his merriest and proved the life of the party.

When the refreshments were over, he insisted that the flour box be brought in and passed around so that every one present might see how much of its contents remained.

"Ladies and gentlemen—if there be any such

present," he declaimed, as the box of flour was gravely passed about the circle. "That which you have the privilege of gazing upon this evening, undoubtedly seems to you merely an humble container of wheat flour, that excellent and fundamental food stuff, so necessary to the sustaining of human life.

"But you are wrong—I cannot impress upon you too much how wrong you are. For this is no ordinary flour box——"

"Sit down there, Elton."

"Who wound you up, anyway?"

"Eat another biscuit and you'll feel better!"

These and other taunts of a like nature had no effect whatever upon the orator.

"But the most baffling, most insoluble mystery of the present day!" he continued. "We are depending upon this lady, whose culinary skill we can all attest, to solve this riddle for us. Ladies and gentlemen, I thank you!" He bowed right and left to a splattering of applause and a good deal of good-natured raillery.

Hugh Draper kept very close to Helen's side during the greater part of the evening, regardless of protests of other youths of the party against his selfishness.

Hugh wore a crisscrossed piece of court plaster over the cut on his forehead. Aside from this, he bore no mark of his meeting with the mysterious stranger.

"The detectives haven't found out anything yet," he said once, in response to a question from Helen. "I have a notion they won't in a hurry, either. The fellow that gave me this little remembrance," fingering the court plaster, "is a pretty cunning old boy, let me tell you, and it will take more than ordinary methods to handle him."

"I hope you aren't planning to set any more traps for him," said Helen anxiously. "I don't want you killed."

"If I meet that fellow again," said Hugh grimly, "*I* won't be the one killed!"

During the evening Rose confided to Joe Morris something concerning her troubles at the store and the tyranny of Henry Goos.

Joe was comfortingly indignant and promised that dire things should befall the floorwalker.

"Leave it to Joe," he told her boastfully. "I cooked that Herbert Shomberg's goose—"

"And now you'll do the same to Henry Goos," dimpled Rose, and immediately swung him off into a fox trot. "Annabelle is a marvel at the piano," she sighed happily. "A cripple would dance to her jazz."

The party broke up at last, as all good things must eventually come to an end, and the young folks departed, assuring their hostesses that the evening had been one "whirl of joy."

"It was fun," remarked Rose. "Now,

Margy, if you could only come to the end of the flour box and solve that mystery for us, we could have nothing more to ask for.''

"I'll *never* come to the end of that flour box," sighed Margy. "I don't believe it has an end!"

The girls were suddenly startled by a pounding on their door.

Before reaching the street entrance Dale Elton had turned and rushed up the stairs. He called now for Margy, and detained her at her apartment door long enough to ask wistfully:

"Won't you let me put just a little column about this in the paper?"

Margy shook her head.

"Just a little paragraph, then?"

Another shake of the head.

"A little line—"

"Not a little word!" cried Margy while, behind her, Rose giggled. "And now, if you don't get out of here, Dale Elton, I will have to call somebody and have you put out."

"I don't believe he has a home," chuckled Rose.

"Some people," said Dale sadly, as he slowly closed the door upon himself, "have not the slightest idea of hospitality. *Au revoir*, my dears—I will see you anon!"

The day after the party Margy sat down on impulse and wrote to J. Jones, Attorney, telling him that the flour was almost used up.

As soon as the mail could bring it to her, she received the lawyer's answer. Margy opened the letter with trembling fingers, wondering if, at last, she was to learn something concerning her inheritance.

Once more she was doomed to disappointment. The lawyer wrote simply that Aunt Margaret Blythe had given no definite directions, merely stating that, when the time came, her niece would find out for herself all she needed to know concerning her inheritance.

"More mystery!" thought Margy, as she tried in vain to get her mind down to the usually interesting business of Miss Pepper's correspondence. "If I don't find out something more about this ridiculous inheritance pretty soon, I will be good for nothing. Why, I can't even attend to my work!"

Meanwhile, the chill of late autumn was setting in in earnest, and the girls were thankful for the comfort of their warmer clothes.

Conditions were no better for Rose at the Lossar-Martin store, and Birdie's drooping figure and lusterless eyes were a constant anxiety to her.

The floorwalker's enmity toward herself increased to such an extent as to be almost intolerable. Rose thought seriously, at last, of resigning her position. She felt that it was only a matter of days, anyway, before Henry Goos would find some excuse for discharging her, and she favored the resignation as a far more dignified mode of exit.

When she confided this decision to Joe—who, in his spare time, had taken to shadowing the floorwalker—the latter was vehement in his protests against what he termed her "foolishness."

"Whatever you do, don't resign. That would be just admitting you were defeated," he argued.

"But if I am discharged—"

"You won't be discharged," Joe assured her, with a lordly gesture. "I'll fix this fellow if I have to go to Mr. Beadle again and give him my opinion on his taste in floorwalkers. First he picks Herbert Shomberg—then Henry Goos! I feel sorry for him, that's all. And if Beadle won't do anything about it, then I'll have it out with the store manager, Paul Caruthers."

"And I feel sorry for you if you do," Rose assured him ruefully.

She was by no means convinced of the wisdom of leaving everything to Joe, as he advised. On the other hand, one hesitates to give up a good position, especially with winter coming on, if one is not absolutely forced to. So Rose decided to trust to luck—and Joe—for a short time longer.

Meanwhile, in spite of the constant trepidation at being left alone in the apartment since the strange things that had happened there,

Helen finally managed to complete her new picture.

One fine fall morning when the air held a tang that set the blood to tingling, she took her latest effort, together with the finished prints, downtown to the shop of Mr. Bullard.

The old gentleman greeted her with his usual cordiality and went over the prints rapidly.

"The prints are very good," he said. "And by the way, I have news for you. Your 'Isle o' Dreams' has been sold. I got forty dollars for it. So I will pay you that amount, less my commission."

"Forty dollars! Oh, that's splendid!" cried Helen, her face beaming.

"And now for your new picture," the art dealer went on. "I am anxious to see it—to make sure your 'Isle o' Dreams' was not just a flash in the pan, so to speak. Eh—what's this?"

He had taken the new picture from the wrappings, was holding it out at arm's length, studying it. Helen watched him, the queer breathlessness that always assailed her at moments like this clutching at her throat.

" 'Alone,' you have called your picture, eh?" Mr. Bullard spoke softly, half to himself, and Helen had to strain to catch the words. "This giant tree away by itself, dwarfing the smaller trees by its majestic height; yet, there is pathos in its very majesty—its aloofness—"

"Oh, you do understand! You see what I have tried to put there," cried Helen, her eyes shining. "I thought it might be necessary to explain—"

"My dear child, the real artist never needs explain the thought behind his picture," the old dealer told her gravely. "It is there, written in each stroke of the brush, for all to read. That is what makes me believe in you, for you have that rare gift, the ability to paint your thought upon the canvas. And," he added with his pleasant smile, "you have the thoughts, as well!"

The result of that interview was to send Helen into the seventh heaven of delight. Not only did Mr. Bullard accept her new picture, but he ordered others.

"The snow will be here soon," he reminded her, as she left. "There will be many beautiful snow scenes in the park. I am anxious to see the first of your winter pictures."

Her thoughts filled with happiness and with gratitude toward this good friend who had helped her so royally, Helen scarcely noticed the ride uptown and was very much surprised to run into Margy at the head of the subway stairs.

"For goodness' sake," said the latter, grabbing her by the arm and hurrying her down the street. "I have been waiting here for ages.

If you hadn't come pretty soon, I'd have gone
and told a perfect stranger—"

"What on earth are you raving about?"
cried Helen, mystified and a bit alarmed. It
was evident that Margy was intensely excited
about something.

"I slipped home, baked up the rest of the
flour and at the bottom of the box, under a false
bottom of pasteboard—"

"Yes!" breathed Helen.

"I found this!" With a dramatic gesture,
Margy held out a square, white envelope.
"From Aunt Margaret Blythe!"

CHAPTER XXIII

CAUGHT

"A LETTER!" cried Helen. "Good stars, Margy, tell me, quick—what does it say?"

"Read for yourself!" directed Margy, and thrust the envelope into her sister's hand.

It is always hard to read anything in the street with people continually passing and jogging one's elbow. Add to this the fact that excitement blurred the words on the page that Helen tried to read, and that Aunt Margy Blythe's handwriting had never been extremely legible at the best of times, and one can readily understand Helen's difficulty in grasping the meaning of that letter.

However, one paragraph did stand out with reasonable clearness, and that was the most important paragraph of all. This was the message Helen caught from the eccentric jumble of phrases.

"Treasure the sofa and the family clock. Look over them carefully. They may contain your inheritance."

Helen stared at her sister and thrust the letter back toward her.

"Have you looked in the furniture?" she asked, quivering with excitement.

"I had a strange feeling about that clock," said Margy, reddening with embarrassment at the admission. "I didn't want to touch it or the furniture, until I had some one to back me up—morally, of course."

"Then, let's hurry!" cried Helen, almost breaking into a run as they neared their corner. "It's—it's the queerest thing I ever heard of, Margy Blythe!"

"Does it occur to you," Margy panted at her shoulder, "that there may be some connection between this letter of Aunt Margy's and the fact that our apartment has been twice entered by a crazy man who seemed to enjoy throwing furniture around?"

"The man may not be so crazy as we thought," her sister replied. "He was probably after your inheritance, Margy. I—I never was so excited in my life!"

"You'd better not expect too much," cautioned Margy. "Chances are if we find anything at all, it will be a thimble or something. I say!" stopping short, as they turned the corner of the street upon which their apartment house was located, "I wonder what all the excitement is about."

"Why, there is a crowd before the house!"

cried Helen, in alarm. "Some one must be hurt!"

The two girls hurried along, elbowing their way through the crowd that hung curiously about the door of the house.

Two policemen were stationed at the door to keep the curious from entering and would have excluded Helen and Margy also had they not lived in the house.

The lower hall was quiet enough, but the girls heard voices overhead. They hurried upstairs, their anxiety growing.

"It's on the fourth floor!" cried Helen suddenly. "Margy—the trouble must be in our flat!"

A strange man came from the door of their apartment, gave the girls a keen, quick glance and hurried past them. Helen would have stopped the man to ask him what had happened, but Margy put a hand on her sister's arm.

"Come on!" she urged. "We'd better see for ourselves."

At the door of their apartment they stopped, eying the scene with consternation.

Several people were in the living room and they were all talking at once. A big burly man, note book in hand, was asking questions of a young fellow whose back was turned to the two girls.

"That's Hugh Draper!" cried Helen, grasping Margy's arm.

"And look what's back of him on the sofa!" said the latter, in a low tone.

With a quickly stifled cry of surprise and fright, Helen recognized the limp form of a man, half sitting, half lying on the sofa at one end of the room.

The man's eye was puffed and swollen and was slowly turning an unpleasant, greenish blue and his lip was cut and bleeding. But by the upstanding mop of sandy-colored hair Helen recognized him immediately as the man she had seen on the stairs following the first intrusion of their apartment and the one, she was sure, who was responsible for Hugh's injury and for days and nights of uneasiness on the part of them all.

At the moment Hugh turned, saw the two girls standing in the doorway, and came toward them with outstretched hand.

"Welcome to our city," he cried, beaming upon them. "The spoils of war are ours. Behold!" He waved a hand toward the couch and the man upon it squirmed uneasily, glaring at them.

"Looks like there had been a war, sure enough," chuckled the big, burly man who had been making notes in his book. "You must have landed a couple of classy uppercuts, young fellow, from the looks of him."

"I sure swung a wicked right," the young lawyer admitted, with justifiable pride.

"Didn't I tell you," he added, turning to Helen, "that the next time I met that nut, said nut would get the worst of it?"

"Wonder you didn't get killed just the same," again interposed the burly man, who, it proved later, was a detective from headquarters. "When I first caught sight of him your friend on the lounge was waving a gun."

The girls had been looking on in a state of dazed bewilderment. Suddenly Helen regained her power of speech.

"You said he had a gun?" she asked of the burly man. The latter obligingly produced a pistol, from which Helen instinctively shrank away. "Hugh—he might have shot you!"

"He certainly might if I hadn't got in my innings first," replied Hugh cheerfully.

"No one has told us a single thing, really, about how this thing happened," Margy broke in impatiently.

While the burly man conferred with his associates and the prisoner glared at them all, Hugh told the two girls what had happened during the last crowded hour.

"It was just by accident that I was here at all," he said. "At the office I found that I had left some important briefs at home and I had to come uptown to get them.

"I had just entered the apartment when I heard a sound overhead and, glancing up, thought I saw some one disappear quickly and furtively around the bend of the stairs.

"On a chance, I followed and reached the fourth floor just in time to see the fellow slip inside your apartment—"

Helen shivered.

"Then he *had* a pass key," she rather stated than asked.

Hugh nodded.

"He seems to have been prepared for all sorts of emergencies. I didn't give him a chance to hide behind a curtain this time," he continued. "Besides, I was afraid he would put up the chain on the inside.

"As a matter of fact, he was just about to do this when I flung the door open and sent him staggering back into the living room.

"There he tripped over a chair, lost his balance, and sprawled his length on the floor. I must say for him, though, that he was as quick as a cat with his hands. Before he had fairly regained his feet he had whipped out a revolver. That," Hugh explained, with a delighted grin, "got me mad!"

"I can't bear to think of it!" cried Helen.

"Go on!" urged Margy, intent upon the story.

"I fell on him," said Hugh. "We mixed it up pretty for a few minutes during which a bullet or two lodged itself in your side walls.

The shots brought the crowd, of course, and the police.

"When they all burst in here, I had hit our friend here a couple of uppercuts and was just in the act of relieving him of his weapon."

"She robbed me, I tell you," suddenly cried the man on the couch in a harsh, loud voice. "She was rich—that Blythe woman—and she robbed a poor man of all his money. That money is here—here, in this furniture in this room! Let me up! I will have what is mine!"

He darted toward the grandfather's clock, ticking in a corner of the room, as though, regardless of his manacled hands, he would once more search its interior for the riches he believed were hidden there.

Two men sprang forward and forced him back upon the couch.

"Get back there, you!" cried one of the men, a small, red-faced man with a beetling brow and piercing black eyes. "Every yip from you from now on, will add two years to your sentence. Get me?"

In response to a tacit question of the girls, Hugh explained that the red-faced man was a Mr. Hicks, a police detective from Des Moines who, for some time, had been trailing John Farrel, the sandy-haired man.

Hugh characterized the latter as a "plain nut" and told them that he had learned from

Hicks that the fellow was wanted on several counts in Iowa.

"It has become a habit with him, it seems," said Hugh, "to get people to go into business with him or invest in some of his crazy schemes. Women were his victims mostly, and your Aunt Margy was the last of them, I guess—although I imagine the old lady was too canny to allow herself to get in very deep."

"But he just said it was Aunt Margy who took his money," Margy reminded him.

"That's just it! As soon as the venture goes under, as it always does, of course, with him running it, he accuses his partner of stealing the 'company's' funds. A couple of times he has got himself in such trouble that he's been forced to run to cover and hide himself for a while."

"This time he didn't get away," said Helen, looking curiously at the prisoner.

"No," agreed Hugh. "And as far as I can make out from Hicks," he added, with a laugh, "the authorities won't know what to do with him now they've got him. They won't know whether to imprison him for fraud or put him in an insane asylum."

"It's a pity," said Helen, with unusual severity, "that they can't do both!"

CHAPTER XXIV

A Fortune

"What do you want done with him, Miss?"

It was the burly man who approached Helen with the question. He jerked a thumb over his shoulder. The two plain-clothes men had pulled the prisoner to his feet and were standing, each with a hand on his shoulder, while the detective, Hicks, waited expectantly.

Helen looked appealingly at Hugh.

"He wants to know if you care to enter a complaint," Hugh explained in answer to the look.

"Oh, I don't know," hesitated Helen. "If he is wanted for other crimes—"

"And some much more serious than this, Miss," broke in Hicks, with a glance at the prisoner.

"Well, then, I think I won't make a complaint against him," said Helen. "If you will just take him away, please—"

She turned away and the burly detective made a sign to the two men who had the prisoner in charge. The group turned right about face and marched toward the door.

When they came opposite the old clock the
prisoner made a dash for it, so sudden and
quick that his captors had all they could do to
retain their grip upon him.

"Here, none of that, sonny!" commanded
Hicks. "Now get out of here, quick!"

The door slammed behind them.

Left alone, the three in the room stared at
each other for a minute. Then Margy and
Helen sank limply down on the couch and Hugh
drew a chair close to them.

"Wow!" he said, taking out a handkerchief
and mopping his forehead. "That was some
session. And say," his face was boyishly
eager, "that fellow put up a good fight!"

"Came near to being your last, too," Margy
reminded him. "Hello, who's this?"

The door opened and Rose stood on the
threshold. She was flushed from hurrying and
her eyes bright with excitement.

"What's all the fuss about?" she demanded.
"There's a crowd in front of the house and
just as I came up, two little men dumped a six-
footer into the patrol wagon. I just caught a
glimpse of the prisoner, but I saw enough to
make sure he had fair hair—"

"Come over here, child," commanded Margy
resignedly. "I see we shall have to tell this
whole thing over again. Sit down here between
Helen and me, and Hugh will tell you all about

his detective work and the trouble it got him into.''

Hugh obligingly related the whole thing to Rose who grew more and more excited as the story progressed.

''Sounds too interesting for real life!'' she commented, when he had finished. ''Pity Dale Elton couldn't have been here. He'd have had the whole thing in the paper by this time.''

''Lucky for him he stayed away!'' snorted Margy. ''It's a wonder he didn't smell out the news and come bounding after it like a cat after a mouse. I never saw such a fellow!''

''Well, thank goodness that desperado is out of the way,'' sighed Rose. ''I won't have to lie awake any more nights, listening for footsteps in the hall. But say,'' she cried, sitting up straight and waving her arms in a gesture of triumph, ''I've got a little good news of my own that I almost forgot about in the excitement. Henry Goos is discharged!''

''No!'' cried Helen and Margy together.

''Yes!'' said Rose, mimicking their tone. ''And Joe Morris did it!''

She went on to explain that Joe had urged her to get up a statement, signed by all the girls in her department, in which a protest was made against the unfair treatment of them by Henry Goos. To this petition was added some facts about Goos that Joe had ferreted out that were not to the man's credit.

This had been presented to Mr. Paul Caruthers, the store manager.

"We learned only to-day that Mr. Caruthers
was so impressed by the 'unanimous protest,'
as he calls it, that he decided to ask for
Goosey's resignation," finished Rose.

"If they don't put some one just as bad in
his place, it will be all right," remarked Margy
pessimistically.

"Oh, that's the best part of it," Rose assured
her. "We are to have an American in the place
now and a fine fellow. One of the girls who
knew him before she came to Lossar-Martin
says he's a prince. From now on Birdie North
may have a chance for her life—to say nothing
of the rest of us. Oh, girls, I am so glad I won't
have to lose my position!"

"Good gracious!" cried Margy, jumping
up so suddenly that she almost upset the other
two on the couch. "Get up out of that chair
Hugh Draper! I almost forgot about my inheritance! Don't you know you may be sitting
on a million dollars?"

Hugh stared and Rose began to clamor at
once for information.

For answer Margy thrust the letter in her
hand—the same she had found at the bottom
of the flour box.

"Read that!" she cried. "Don't ask questions. I haven't time to answer them."

She rushed into the kitchen and returned a

minute later, vigorously brandishing the carving knife.

Hugh, who had been reading the letter with Rose, stepped to one side with alacrity.

"Can't I do that?" he asked politely, as Margy made as though ruthlessly to rip up the haircloth rocker.

"You can—but may not!" retorted Margy, grinning up at him. "I don't have a fortune left me every day, and I'm not going to be done out of the fun of looking for it. Get out of my way everybody, if you don't want to be sliced in half!"

In spite of this fearful threat, Rose made a dash for the grandfather's clock, only to be intercepted by the knife-brandishing Margy.

"If you touch that clock, Rose Blythe, I'll have your life! Please let me do this my way, just for this once," she pleaded in a different tone. "I have a terrible hankering to be the first to lay hands on my inheritance, even if it should prove to be only a brass thimble—or a canary bird."

"It should be a cuckoo, if it lived in the clock," chuckled Rose. Nevertheless, she obligingly stood aside to watch Margy ruin the haircloth rocker.

But here Helen interfered.

"There's no use ruining the chair, Margy. Rose, go for the tack hammer. Bring the big screwdriver, too, honey. It will do to punch

and poke with. Hugh, you lift the chair over
—with its legs in the air. We can rip the bottom cloth off and get into the springs and
stuffing that way. We'll take the covering off
the back of the chair, too."

Rose and Hugh Draper hastened to do
Helen's bidding, and Margy very quickly had
the lining off the bottom of the seat.

Although Margy searched the old chair thoroughly, nothing came to light and she turned a
troubled face to her eager audience.

"Nothing here," she announced. "Now, I
wonder—"

"But, Margy, Aunt Margaret says nothing
in this letter about either of the chairs!" Helen
had picked up the letter where Rose had
dropped it in her excitement and had read
it through again. "Listen! She says, 'treasure the sofa and the family clock.'"

"Well, of all the idiots!" cried Margy,
abandoning the chair and making a dash for the
clock. "Wasting valuable time on this old
thing!"

Margy opened the face of the clock. Helen,
Hugh, and Rose peered eagerly over her shoulder. But there was certainly no place there
that could contain a treasure, however small
and compact.

"Hugh, come help me, please!" cried Margy,
with growing impatience. "I want to get the

old clock down on its face so I can look in the back.''

Hugh turned the clock down on its face so that they might examine the back of it.

''Aren't you glad you came?'' asked Rose of Hugh, with an impish smile. ''Just so Margy can wish all the heavy work on you?''

The young lawyer grinned, but did not reply. He was watching Margy's slim fingers busily exploring the back of the old clock.

''Perhaps there is some secret spring,'' he suggested.

''Don't you suppose I have thought of that?'' cried Margy, in exasperation. ''I have felt over every square inch of the old thing—Hello! what's this?''

''This'' was the gentle whir and twang of a released spring, and before the eyes of the astonished watchers a shallow drawer, well hidden far down in the body of the clock, slid slowly open.

Rose gave a little scream of excitement and surprise, while Helen nearly pushed Margy into the clock in her eagerness to see what was inside the little receptacle.

There was a long envelope within the drawer. Margy drew it forth with shaking fingers and, having turned it about in every possible position, spread it out where they all could see.

Across the front of it was scrawled in Aunt Margaret Blythe's illegible handwriting,

"To my niece and namesake, Margaret
Blythe. Her inheritance."

"Well, open it!" cried Rose, in a fever of impatience. "Don't sit there staring at it, Margy
Blythe!"

CHAPTER XXV

The Snowstorm

Slowly Margy opened the envelope. Her eyes were big and dark and in her cheeks burned two spots of feverish color. From the envelope she drew forth two long heavy slips of paper.

In her eagerness Rose would have taken the papers from her. But Margy held them away from her, scrambled to her feet, and went over to the window.

"Girls," she cried, turning to them as they eagerly followed her, "these are Liberty Bonds! Liberty Bonds, do you hear? And they are for five hundred dollars—"

"Five hundred dollars!" echoed Rose ecstatically. "I never hoped to see so much money all together at one time before I died—"

"But you don't understand," cried Margy, waving the Liberty Bonds wildly before her. "The bonds are for five hundred dollars apiece! And they've got, oh! so many coupons attached!"

"A thousand dollars!" Rose threw up her

hand and collapsed upon the couch. "Oh, this is too much! Fan me, somebody, quick!"

Margy seized Helen by the waist and whirled her about the room in a sort of fantastic two step.

"A thousand dollars! A thousand dollars!" she chanted. "I'm a wealthy woman! I'm a wealthy woman! I'll buy me a house and an automobile—"

"Let me go, crazy thing!" cried Helen, half choked with laughter and excitement. "Hugh, will you make her let go? She's pulling me to pieces!"

Hugh obligingly caught Margy in the midst of a wild whirl and brought her to a sharp right-about-face. He held her firmly by both shoulders and spoke severely.

"Now, young lady, will you please listen to me a minute?"

"And who are you?" cried Margy, making an impudent face at him.

"Never mind!" replied Hugh scowling prodigiously. "And you needn't think you can talk back to a future judge of the Supreme Court, even if you have just become an heiress. Now you listen to me—"

"I'm listening!" interrupted Margy, with mock humility.

"Good! Now then, for a young person possessed of unusual intelligence—"

"Much obliged!" murmured Margy.

"I find it hard to credit the fact," Hugh went on, unmoved, "that you should have overlooked an item of singular importance!"

"Which is—" prompted Margy.

"That you have not yet finished the search for your inheritance—"

"Bless the man!" cried Margy, with an explosive chuckle. "He actually thinks that I have forgotten the sofa. Don't make me laugh, Hugh Draper. Is anybody coming with me?"

She made a dash for the door, holding the precious bonds clutched tight in her hand. The others followed her hilariously.

It was Helen who brought them up short before the door of the Drapers' flat.

"Perhaps your mother won't want us to come in just now," she said to Hugh, hesitating; but the latter brushed aside her objections.

"She will be only too glad to share the fun," he assured her. "She has really been filled with curiosity concerning this inheritance, though she wouldn't admit the fact."

However, Helen insisted that he go in first and prepare his mother for the "onslaught."

Mrs. Draper herself came back with her son and flung the door wide for them.

"You foolish children, even to think you must ask to come in for such a purpose," she said, and the girls saw that she was flushed and her eyes were bright. "Come in at once. I am as eager as you to see what the old sofa contains.''

"If anything!" qualified Margy.

But she was really not in the least pessimistic, which was proved a moment later by the hearty way in which she fell upon the old sofa. She had left her own tack hammer upstairs, but Hugh willingly supplied another.

It seemed at first as though this part of the search were to prove fruitless. Although Margy poked and prodded inside the ancient piece of furniture, she got nothing but a few scratches—of which she complained petulantly.

"Here, let me try," cried Rose, at last, unable to stand the suspense any longer. "If two heads are better than one, I don't see why two hands shouldn't be!"

"Yes, and two cooks often spoil the broth, too," grumbled Margy. "Wait a minute!" An eager look sprang to her eyes and she plunged her arm still deeper into the interior of the couch. "I think I feel something. There, I've gone and pushed it further down!"

"Oh, you do it, Hugh, you have longer arms!" cried Rose, dancing with impatience.

"I've got it!" cried Margy triumphantly, and while they crowded about she produced another envelope. As far as could be seen by the exterior, it was identical in every way to the one found in the clock. Even the inscription was the same.

There was intense quiet while Margy solemnly drew forth the contents of the envelope.

"Liberty Bonds again!" breathed Rose.

Margy nodded.

"Only this time there are three of them, instead of two!"

"Of the same denomination?" asked Helen, in a whisper, too excited to speak in a natural tone.

Again Margy nodded.

"Fifteen hundred dollars!" Margy spoke incredulously. "And, with the thousand added, it makes twenty-five hundred dollars! Girls, I can't believe it. Dear old Aunt Margy. I believe—good gracious, I am afraid I'm going to —cry!"

And this she did whole-heartedly, with Helen's arms about her and Rose patting her shoulder comfortingly. It was such an unaccustomed thing to see Margy cry that no one knew just what to do about it.

"I was thinking of Aunt Margy," her namesake explained rather shamefacedly, as she dabbed at her eyes with her handkerchief. "Poor old soul—she must have been so lonesome! I was wishing that I might get her back for a moment, long enough to say thank you!"

Of course all the friends and acquaintances of the girls had to know of Margy's good for-

tune. They flocked about her, showering her
with congratulations and good wishes and suggestions as to how she should dispose of her
newly acquired wealth.

Margy laughed at them, telling them that she
intended to put the money in the bank, where
it would be the nucleus, she hoped, of a real fortune.

"Of course I expect to spend some of the interest on the bonds," she told them, laughing.
"I wouldn't be human if I didn't want to have
a little fun out of it right now."

One of the things Margy planned for that
part of her inheritance not put in the bank, had
to do with patient Birdie North and her mother.

"Of course I will have to manage it so they
will never think of me," she said, plotting happily with her sisters. "A hundred dollar bill
sent to them anonymously at Christmas time,
won't arouse their suspicions."

"Even if they should suspect, they never
would be able to pin the awful deed on you,"
said Rose. Then she got up and gave Margy a
bear's hug. "You are a dear to do this for
Birdie, Margy," she said. "That hundred
dollars will seem as big as a mountain to her."

"It will buy some nice things for her mother,
and perhaps pay a doctor's bill," said Margy.
"Brave girl! If ever any one deserves help
and a little bit of sunshine, her name is Birdie
North!"

With the removal of Henry Goos and the arrival of his successor, a splendid, upstanding young American, life once more settled into its usual, happy routine at the Lossar-Martin store. Of course Joe Morris took upon himself all the credit for the changed conditions, but as Rose was inclined to agree with him, there was nothing to quarrel about in that!

Meanwhile Helen painted busily and happily in the restored peace of the little apartment. Hugh Draper came often to see her work, occasionally offering suggestions and helpful criticism and always encouraging her. Never once did his belief in her ability waver.

Happy days for the girls, without a cloud, apparently, upon the horizon of their contentment and ambition. It was wonderful to know that they had accomplished so much in so short a time. They had gained a firm foothold in their respective vocations, and, what was far more important, the girls had made staunch and loyal friends. The inheritance was indeed something to be thankful for, and the girls felt that all the world was kind to them.

Shortly after the finding of Margy's inheritance Helen awoke one Sunday morning to find the outer world a mist of falling snow.

Seeing that some of the snow was drifting through her open window, she got out of bed to shut it. Just then Rose came in.

"The first snowstorm of the season!" Rose cried, as she pushed Helen back into bed and tumbled in after her. It was Sunday morning, and so it was not necessary to get up at once. "Joe suggested that we get up a party and go to the park this afternoon. I don't see why we should stop for the snow, do you?"

They got together their party and repaired to the park, early in the afternoon, defiant of drifting snow and stinging winds.

They found a sheltered corner of the park and ate like Eskimos, huddled in their coats.

"Some biscuits, Margy!" said Lloyd Roberts, consuming his third with gusto. "Did these come from Aunt Margy's flour box?"

"Foolish question!" returned Margy. "You know I used the last of that flour long ago."

"Say, fellows," cried Joe Morris, suddenly standing up and flourishing a sandwich about his head, "I vote we give three cheers for the heiress in our midst—the luckiest girl in America." And cheers were given hilariously.

"Of course, it's all perfectly absurd and foolish," sighed Margy contentedly. "But just now I must say I do feel like the luckiest girl in the world!''

''And the nicest,'' murmured Dale Elton, at her elbow.

Margy chuckled and looked at him thoughtfully. At that moment Margy Blythe was too utterly contented with her lot, even to put Dale Elton in his place.

''Have it your own way,'' she murmured, and reached for another piece of cake.

THE END

www.ingramcontent.com/pod-product-compliance
Lightning Source LLC
Chambersburg PA
CBHW020318260626
47156CB00004B/1268